HALLOWEEN FIEND

C.V. HUNT

GRINDHOUSE PRESS

Grindhouse Press
PO BOX 521
Dayton, Ohio 45401

Grindhouse Press #047
ISBN-10: 1-941918-43-3
ISBN-13: 978-1-941918-43-2

For Andy
I love you more than Halloween.

Other titles by C.V. Hunt

ONE

NO ONE KNEW WHERE HALLOWEEN came from. It had always lived in the town as long as anyone could remember. Most of the townspeople assumed it materialized when the town was built. Others thought the founders must've constructed the town over its home without knowing. Because to think someone would break ground with the knowledge of what would become of the town and its inhabitants was horrific. Only a sadist would intentionally inflict the dreadful things we lived through every day onto innocent people.

I carefully pulled the edge of the dingy, nicotine-stained curtain covering the front door window to the side. I left the slightest slit to peer out at the darkening street. If Halloween was out there I didn't see it and I surely didn't want it to see me. I was safe within the house for the most part but seeing it, seeing it move, unnerved me and sent pinpricks down my spine every time. After forty-five years of living here and knowing I would die here, one would think I would've grown used to it. And for the most part I tried to ignore its existence but for some inexplicable reason I was compelled to listen for it tonight.

A few of the street lights came to life, prompting me to flip the switch for our porchlight. The street was empty and quiet as usual for this time of day. No fools lived here. Or maybe we were all fools.

Everyone would've already made their way home long before the dreaded time of evening when the sun slipped beyond the horizon. The majority of the houses on our street—and most of the town—were dark and vacant. One thing you never saw in Strang was a 'For Sale' sign. The houses were either inhabited or vacant. And once a house was empty it stayed that way. Which wasn't necessarily a bad thing. No one cared about property values. There were more important things to worry about.

The elderly woman who lived across the street, Janice, stood in her front window with the curtains completely open. I never could understand why she chose to leave her damn drapes open at this time of night. She must be sick in the head one way or the other. The cat contained in the cage on Janice's front step was dimly illuminated by her yellowed porchlight. The animal pulled furiously at the corner of the wire door with its cupped paw but was unsuccessful at opening it, which was fortunate for Janice and unfortunate for the animal. Occasionally she'd stop me on my way to or from work to chat and I always made it a point to warn her and try to convince her to switch to something more docile. But she still continued to use cats. I hoped her cage never failed. There weren't many of us still living in Strang, a hundred at most, and not that the way we lived was anything remotely close to normal, but when a cage failed or when a homeowner was unfortunate enough to have forgotten to leave a treat for Halloween, the consequences affected the entire town. It brought a jolt of fear to the surface amongst the townspeople. When you lived a certain way day in and day out you became desensitized to it and complacent and it all became muscle memory. Once there was a hiccup in the routine around Strang everyone became a bit more vigilant and paranoid. It made one take stock in their actions and brought what was really happening here to the forefront of everyone's mind.

I peered down at the guinea pig in the carrier cage on our stoop. It stupidly stared at nothing without a care in the world or the knowledge of what was to come. It worked its jaws around a few pieces of hay I'd given it.

I let the curtain fall back into place but didn't move from the door. Normally I would've made my way to the basement by now but with All Hallows' Eve right around the corner the atmosphere was supercharged. The leaves had begun to turn and drop. The air was crisp and cool and filled with the smells of decaying plants and sleeping earth. You could feel the threat of Old Man Winter and the anxiety and dread of the Halloween holiday approaching. Every year I solidified the oncoming holiday with a glance at the thing that visited every night. I never knew where the compulsion to hear or see the thing came from around this time of year. Maybe it was to celebrate the cheap thrills of horror and fear people from anywhere else ensconced themselves in for the approaching holiday. Like visiting a haunted attraction or watching scary movies or setting out decorations.

The grandfather clock ticked softly but still could be heard over Dad's programs playing at a nearly earsplitting level. The three-quarter chime began, signaling the official twilight for today. The cages of guinea pigs lining the living room wall erupted into squeaks and squeals. I always wondered if the furry things had a sense of what was happening every night or of their impending doom.

Dad laughed at something playing out on the television. His laughter was wet and quickly transformed into a series of hacking coughs. I turned to observe him stub out his cigarette and turn his oxygen tank back on. The hiss and puff of his oxygen joined the dissonance that filled our house nearly every minute of every day. My unspoken theory was Dad couldn't go a second without some type of auditory chaos to fill the deep emptiness of the void within him he'd never admit to having.

Sometimes I wished he'd forget to turn off the tank or maybe not close the valve entirely and blow the whole damn house up when he lit his cigarette. The guy who delivered his medical supplies chastised him every time he spotted his overflowing ashtrays. But Dad had never been concerned with much of anything having to do with safety. For his or anyone around him. If he'd cared one ounce, he wouldn't have taken root in Strang and refused to budge.

There wasn't much to do within the house after sunset other than to argue with Dad over something trivial or watch whatever braindead show he'd managed to pick from one of three channels that reached this godforsaken town. Every day was pretty routine. I would come home, do whatever chores needed attending to, cook, set out the treat for Halloween, and retreat to my room in the basement and try my damnedest to escape into the recesses of my mind. The alternative was to sit around with Dad and listen to him moan and complain about his plight in life and have him tell me how to live my life, which wasn't much of a life to begin with.

I was staring at the floor and lost in thought when Dad craned his head around the back of his recliner and noticed me. "Barry!" he barked. "Get away from the damn door!" His voice was wet and lispy. He refused to wear his false teeth anymore, which made it difficult to understand half the things he said unless he was shouting.

The guinea pigs started another ruckus round of calls, having been startled by Dad's outburst. I turned toward him. I could tell he was impatiently waiting for me to respond so he could turn back to his television. And he'd only taken the time to yell at me because there was a commercial on. He lifted his upper lip to expose his toothless gums. An expression he made to position his slipping glasses at the correct angle to look at me through his bifocals.

"I'm listening," I said. "To make sure."

"You're a demented shit who gets off on killing those things. Why don't you go to your room like normal?"

I shook my head to signal I was disregarding his question and turned back to the door. There was no sense in responding to him. No reason or explanation ever abated him. I literally could not remember how many times we'd had this exact same argument and the thought of answering him made me feel exhausted. I don't think the old man gave a shit whether he lived or died anymore. If I didn't set out the treat every night I was certain he'd let it lapse. And to try and have any type of intellectual conversation with him would throw him into a fit of rage and he would accuse me of trying to make him feel stupid.

He grumbled something. A lot of what he said was incoherent. Once I tried to convince him to wear his teeth, at least, for the benefit of not creeping me out. His argument had been he received limited government assistance and was determined to make the teeth he owned last forever, despite his gums morphing over the extended period he'd gone sans teeth. At this point he couldn't wear them anymore if he wanted.

A scream came from outside and was cut short. My heart leapt into my throat. The sudden fear made my chest feel tight and it became difficult to breathe. There wasn't a time it wasn't startling and disconcerting to hear the squeaks and squeals and squalls of the terrified animals but you learned to tune it out and I'd been distracted by Dad. Most nights, I was in my basement room where the concrete walls blocked the majority of the sounds and what little did filter through was easily covered by Dad's noisy television programs or the record player I kept to play the few LPs I owned. It appeared our street was the first up on Halloween's agenda tonight.

As much as I didn't want to look, I couldn't help myself. The hair on the back of my neck rose as I moved the curtain. I hoped the movement was so slight it wouldn't be detected by Halloween if it happened to be within sight of our house.

The daylight had faded rapidly, leaving the sky a dark blue with hints of pink and yellow along the horizon, casting the street in navy blue shadows. At first glance I spotted the silhouette of a man stooped over the cage on Janice's porch. But the figure blurred and transformed too rapidly for the eye to keep up. The shadow it cast never changed and always kept to the same shape I assumed was its actual form—a thin, hunched figure with an oversized head and long fingers. The shadow appeared to be made out of sharp angles. On the occasions I'd watched it I thought I caught its shadow opening its mouth to reveal plentiful and sharp teeth. As with all shadows the height was indeterminable but I knew it wasn't short. The thing itself shifted again and again to something human then something with possibly tentacles then to something winged or wide, I couldn't be sure. It confused the mind to look directly at it. The shadow was what you had to pay attention to.

As it devoured the cat Janice offered, the shadow turned its head toward our house.

I let go of the curtain and stepped back from the door. I was certain it had seen me. It unnerved me to think Halloween was aware of me. Aware of my curiosity. The thing found pleasure in screwing with people. Tricking people.

Between the nightly offerings, the way it reveled in our fear, the constant shifting of its 'costume', the ritual it fulfilled regardless of our participation every All Hallows' Eve, and its propensity to recite Halloween-themed riddles and rhymes, the townspeople at some point started referring to it as Halloween.

The television, the ticking clock, and the guinea pigs were enough to mask most any noise. But somehow I knew. I wasn't ever sure if it was the actual sound of the thing or if it could somehow make its presence known and the sounds were all in my head. There were no rules while dealing with Halloween. It was as if it made them up as it went along. Like a spoiled child who'd play in the schoolyard as long as it was winning and throw a tantrum the moment it sensed it wasn't going to get what it wanted.

Halloween insistently spoke to itself and others in a hissing whisper of rhymes and riddles. It was an insane babble of nonsense and if you tried to make out anything it was saying it could drive you crazy. Something dark and looming and sinister invaded my senses and I knew it was approaching our house. I could've sworn there was a shift or creak in the steps even over the cacophony within the house.

Then I was certain I heard it. Or at least thought I heard it. I wasn't sure if it was part of the babbling or if it was actually addressing us.

Something dark and menacing said, "Trick or treat."

The sound of its voice—whether it was only in my head or not—made my bones ache with terror. Nausea unsettled my stomach and my chest became tight and painful. I rubbed the ache in my chest mindlessly and kept my eyes glued to the door. I knew I wasn't in the greatest physical shape, evident by the gut hanging over the top of my trousers, and I worried I might end up giving myself a heart attack.

The metal scrape of the cage came from beyond the door, followed by the quick yip of the guinea pig.

Dad burst into a round of laughter along with the laugh track of the television show. He hadn't been paying any attention to tonight's routine other than to yell at me for standing by the door. He was a master of plummeting into his own world and blocking out anything that would interfere with his conceited agenda. The guinea pigs in the house chortled, either with Dad or in response to their distressed companion. Like Dad, the animals never seemed to be bothered by Halloween. They just responded to whatever noise antagonized them. Ignorant creatures with pea brains.

The pain in my chest lessened and I took another step back from the door.

"Trick or treat," it said again.

I couldn't express the sense of dread and fear Halloween evoked. The thin wooden door and the few feet of empty space between it and me were not enough. I spun and dashed across the living room toward the kitchen. My hip hit an old curio cabinet and made its contents jingle.

I wasn't sure if Halloween was speaking directly to me or if that was its normal babble but I had to get away from it. Sometimes I thought I transformed into some sort of masochist around this time of year. But when you were stuck in the living hell that was Strang with nowhere to go you became numb and desensitized from feeling much of anything. Even if it was fear for my life it was better than the dark compliant depression we all dealt with while continuing to walk around with giant smiles on our faces like everything was perfectly normal. But the pain in my chest made me realize playing with fear wasn't a safe option anymore. I was getting too old to use the high of terror for a thrill anymore.

"Where ya goin?!" Dad yelled. "I need help getting into my Jazzy Chair. I gotta take a leak!"

Once in the kitchen I flung open the basement door and lost my grip on the handle. The door bounced off the wall and almost clobbered me as I took the first step.

"If you're not gonna help me into my chair at least bring me the piss jug!"

An instinctual part of me wanted to spin on my heels and help him. The muscle memory of assistance was deep but I knew his helplessness was a ruse and lately I'd grown sick of it. He was perfectly capable of taking care of himself. The man was a pity monger. Using his disabilities to garner sympathy. And even if I wanted to assist him there was nothing that was going to stop me from barricading myself in the basement for the rest of the night. I wanted to be as far away from Halloween as I could get.

I dashed down the stairs to my room and retrieved a random LP. My hands shook furiously as I unsheathed the vinyl and almost dropped the record. I placed the vinyl on the turntable as daftly as my hands would allow and turned the volume up. But no matter where I ran to or how loud I played the music, I could still hear a low chuckling coming from the thing on our front step.

TWO

THE WALK TO THE STORE was cool and damp. October was in full swing and the fog that settled in the town overnight still lingered in the morning hours after the sun had risen. The few cages situated on the stoops of the houses were all empty and disheveled as usual. The fallen leaves made a satisfying but unnerving crunch underfoot in the early morning silence. I spotted a splatter of oxidized blood on the front steps of the Hendrix's place before crossing the street to the church ... or what used to be a church.

A crow sat on the sill of one of the broken stained-glass windows. Its caw was nearly deafening as I passed. The bird set off a half-dozen more of its friends nesting in the non-functioning bell tower. The town wasn't remotely interested in religion anymore and I could barely remember a time when the church was used for its actual purpose instead of a siren to inform the town of any unpalatable occurrences and a place for children to vandalize ... back when there were children in Strang.

I made it to the main two blocks without spotting anyone. The town was deserted like any other day. A few cars were parked along the street. The vehicles belonged to a few older business owners who lived on the outskirts of Strang and didn't quite have it in them to walk the distance anymore. Not that there was much business happening for them to tend to but people at least needed their essentials. The only other option for groceries and whatnot was to drive forty-five minutes to the next town where you wouldn't be able to get much more than what you could pick up in Strang.

Jacob was leaning against his register inside the gas station. He waved a gnarled and arthritic hand when he spotted me. I passed the post office but didn't see Margaret lingering behind the counter as she usually did in the early morning hours. She must have been in back with Arthur, sorting the day's mail and helping him load up before he started delivering.

Most of the storefronts were empty. Some of their windows were covered in brown paper to keep looky-loos from seeing what state of disrepair the place had fallen into. Most of the windows were covered in a thick layer of grime and dust. Some of the panes were cracked, showing the many years they'd been neglected to anyone bothering to notice.

The restaurant was almost deserted except for Old Hurly. He sat stooped at the counter, dipping his toast into runny eggs lackadaisically, staring at nothing while Rhonda leaned against the counter and stared out the front window vacantly. I slowed my stride while passing the restaurant, hoping to catch Rhonda's eye, but she appeared too deep in thought and didn't see me. Which was probably for the better, as I knew any attention or acknowledgment from her would make my face burn with embarrassment. Her red hair appeared extra vibrant and I wondered if she'd newly colored it or was trying a different brand of color. I took the last few seconds of crossing in front of the window to stare at her cleavage so I could store the image away.

I redirected my attention to the store and spotted the orange flyer tacked to the corkboard beside the main entrance. Every year went faster than the previous. And every year when the calendar flipped to October I tried to put it out of my mind and not worry about the upcoming events until the orange paper appeared again and the inevitable was in motion. Once I reached the corkboard I stopped to read the flyer:

Strang Fall Festival
When: All Hallows' Eve
Time: Noon - ?

Events: Horseshoe competition, costume contest, haunted
hayride, and more!
Food and beer!
New this year! Thrill rides from Wacky Times Amusements!
Town meeting this Friday.

"Thrill rides?" I mumbled and shook my head.

I pulled the handle for the door of the store and the bell rang to signal a customer. The clock on the wall showed I'd arrived five minutes early. Kathy sat on the stool by the register with her arms folded, looking disgruntled, which wasn't anything different from any other day.

Mr. McCallister poked his head out of the office door beyond the deli to the right of the front door. Beyond the deli was a small makeshift room housing the VHS rentals.

"Barry?" Mr. McCallister said.

I waved at him. "Here, mister McCallister."

"I'll write down your time." He disappeared back into the office.

I approached the only register in the store. Kathy glared at me as I retrieved my employee vest from under the stainless-steel table where the groceries were bagged.

"Fall Festival's comin'," she said.

Her statement was part accusatory, as if I'd had something to do with the situation, and part stating the obvious. I could never be sure what was implied when Kathy spoke since her brow was constantly furrowed, regardless of what mood she was in. Everything she said felt like a trap. Either into an argument or into a conversation you didn't really want to be a participant in. The thought of talking to her always made me feel exhausted before the conversation even began.

"Yeah," I responded. I always added a note of annoyance when responding to her, hoping she'd take the hint I didn't want to talk.

"Got thrill rides this year."

Again, I wasn't sure what she wanted from me or where the conversation was going, but since she felt the need to address the event, I was certain she was about to spend the rest of the day ranting to anyone who'd listen to her.

"Yeah," I said. I pulled on my employee vest, noting it was progressively getting tighter with my slowly expanding belly.

Keeping her arms crossed, she stretched her neck in my direction before spitting, "That all you can say? Yeah. Yeah."

"What do you want me to do about it?"

She threw her arms up, frustrated. "Well, hell. I don't know. Something! The whole place is going to hell in a handbasket! The place is gonna be swarming with *carnies*." She spat the last word in a derogatory tone.

"Language!" Mr. McCallister called from the office.

"There's no customers!" Kathy barked back.

I chuckled. "I think carnival rides are the least of our worries." I pulled my shoulders tighter, hoping to stretch the fabric of the vest, but immediately began to worry I'd rip the ugly garment.

"They don't know 'bout what's goin' on here. Where they gonna stay? What're we gonna tell them?"

"I'm sure that's all been figured out. I don't think they'd arrange it without having all the kinks worked out."

"Has it been worked out, mister know-it-all?"

I waved at her dismissively and the material of the vest squeezed around my shoulders with the gesture. I swore the vest was now a few sizes too small. Mr. McCallister hadn't seen a reason to order a new one for me yet even though I could no longer button the thing and a few seams were coming unraveled. It had been almost thirty years since he'd given it to me and I was starting to wonder if he was waiting for me to die so he wouldn't have to replace it, or waiting for himself to die, or if once I was gone he'd pass it on to the next employee and the damn thing would be worn until it disintegrated.

I said, "Maybe you should be a part of the planning committee if you're so concerned." I turned and started down one of the aisles, heading toward the back to retrieve the few boxes needing shelved.

"Ain't no one got no goddamn time for that! Sun's settin' earlier an' earlier!"

"Language!" Mr. McCallister called.

I didn't have much time for it either with the days getting shorter. Dad would make my life a bigger living hell than what it already was if I decided to have any extracurricular activity that didn't involve him or wasn't centered around him. I wouldn't admit it to

Kathy but I was curious too. How were they going to deal with a group of people from out of town? Where would they stay? And I was certain I wouldn't be the only looky-loo if I could manage to drag Dad to the town meeting.

THREE

"TOWN MEETING ON FRIDAY," I said as I closed the front door. I sat one of the grocery sacks with guinea pig food on the floor by the cages.

Dad was rooted to his recliner watching television, as usual, with a smoldering cigarette in hand. Half of his cigarette was ashes and the ashes were curved and threatening to fall onto the floor. There was a growing pile of ashes from the other smokes he'd had today beside his chair even though an ashtray sat six inches from his elbow on an end table. The table was covered with half a dozen empty soda cans. Without turning from his programs he said, "I'm not going."

"You should." I crossed the living room with the remaining groceries, retrieved a carton of cigarettes from one of the bags, and sat the carton on the end table beside him. Before entering the kitchen I stopped and said, "It's October."

I'd set the food on the counter before he'd had a chance to let what I'd said sink in.

"It ain't October!" he called.

"Yeah it is."

He grunted and huffed and I knew he was making his way to his Jazzy Chair. I unpacked the spaghetti noodles, hamburger, tomato sauce, and the generic packet of dried spaghetti sauce seasoning. I had the water on the stove to boil and had begun browning the hamburger before he made his first attempt to pass through the doorway. The front right bumper of his chair hit the doorjamb. He kept gunning the small electric engine. The chair dug its millionth gouge into the wood as he tried to force the chair into the kitchen instead of backing up, realigning the machine, and trying again. The Jazzy Chair was only halfway through the doorway before he began rocking in the seat, trying to budge it further, before huffing and puffing in frustration and giving up.

He said, "There's no way it's October."

"Yes it is, Dad. If you left the house for more than your yearly doctor's appointment and the occasional town meeting you'd notice the seasons changing. Hell, if you looked out the window every now and then you'd know what time of year it is."

"I'm an old man. I'm on disability. I can't be going outside—"

I waved a hand dismissively at him. "Yeah. Yeah. Yeah. I know."

"What day is it?"

"Tuesday."

"Are they having the fall festival this year?"

"Have they ever not?"

He grumbled something I didn't understand.

I said, "They have amusement rides this year."

"Amusement rides? What for? The last thing we need is a circus. They act like this is some kind of goddamn celebration! Are they gonna have a parade too?"

I shrugged. "I don't think it's a circus. Just a few rides."

"Who's gonna run 'em? Who's gonna *ride* them? I sure as hell ain't. Does it look like I can get on a ride?"

I shrugged again.

"Is that all you can do?" He began shrugging spastically over and over. "You look like you have epilepsy."

I spoke louder and harsher than intended. "I guess you'll have to go to the meeting to find out, won't you?"

"Gah!" He put his chair in reverse but it was still hung up on the doorway. "You can't yell at me. I'm your dad." He began throwing himself against the chair back, trying to dislodge it. "You can't wait for the meeting. You want your old man to get the dot, don't ya?" He stopped and his eyes brightened. "Do you think they'll give dots to the circus people? Maybe it's a ruse to give one of them the dot."

"I don't want you to get the dot. I don't want anyone to get the dot." I sat the spoon on the counter and approached him. I grabbed the handle of his chair and gave it a hard shove to dislodge it from the doorjamb. He huffed a few times as if he'd been the one to exert the physical strength to move the chair. "Would you go back in the living room and let me cook dinner? I'll bring it to you when it's ready."

He hit the power button for the chair and backed into the wall of the small hallway leading to the bathroom, his bedroom, and Mom's bedroom, which sat in the same state it'd been in when she died. He put the chair gear in the forward position before making a several point turn around in the living room, clipping all the furniture as he went. Once he got the chair pointed in the general direction of the hallway he said, "Gotta take a leak. And don't you go draining the fat off that burger before adding the sauce. The grease is the best part."

I returned to the food on the stove as he drove into the hallway wall. I could hear him grunting and knew he was rocking in the chair, trying to straighten it. There was a prolonged scraping as he forced the chair down the hallway wall toward the bathroom.

FOUR

I FED THE GUINEA PIGS after dinner while Dad was in the bathroom. I tried to feed a Brussels sprout to one of the pregnant sows I'd separated from the others. She was nestled in the corner of her cage and refused the offer. She had to be getting close to delivering.

The grandfather clock chimed and signified it was getting close to dusk. I moved down the line of cages toward the adult males. A handful of males were more than enough to keep the females pregnant. The animals were restless but silent today. I opened the door for the bulls and blindly selected one.

I didn't want to know which one. I didn't want to make eye contact with it. I didn't want to think of what its fate was or what my next few actions meant for the poor creature. There was a time I tried to apologize for what I was about to do or thank them for their sacrifice but I found acknowledging any of it was depressing. You had to learn to keep emotions separate early on because the moment you grew an ounce of empathy for anyone or anything, the night Halloween paid a visit you would end up in a constant state of grief and sorrow and depression. Because Halloween doesn't leave until it got what it came for and there are no takebacks.

Dad made distressed noises that could be heard over the television as he used the restroom. I checked the clock again as I placed the guinea pig in the outdoor cage and gave the bull a few pieces of hay. I opened the front door and set the contraption on the step. The yowl of the cat on Janice's porch drew my attention. Janice stood in her window with an enthusiastic smile on her face, as usual. She waved at me and I waved back before shutting the door.

I didn't know how Janice could stand to watch out the window every night. I guess it was the same morbid curiosity that compelled me to stand at the door and listen this time of year but it happened to be daily for her. I hoped whatever drew me into it every year around this time didn't become a nightly habit. Maybe it was the same fear and fretfulness that filled everyone's mind that caused her to watch every time because I knew at least with me there was always the constant nagging in the back of my mind telling me this day could be the last day. In a perfect world the sentiment of it all coming to an end would be a happy one but that wasn't the case in Strang. There were no happy endings here. Halloween might decide it wasn't happy with our offerings. It might come for Janice tonight. It might come for me. There was nothing stopping it from coming for anyone other than a dubious social contract with an entity no one could trust. And how could such an old woman like Janice stand it? I was a grown man and the thing gave me the heebie-jeebies and made me feel as if I were an elementary kid watching his first horror film.

Come on, Barry, I thought. *Grow some balls. If Janice isn't scared there's no reason for you to act like a pussy.*

I touched the edge of the curtain covering the door window. The clock on the wall read a minute till dusk. I yanked the curtain fully open and stared out the window at the darkening street. Janice leaned on the sill of her window and craned her head back and forth to see up and down the street. She appeared as excited as a child waiting for a playmate to arrive.

The toilet flushed down the hall. The grunts from Dad renewed as he made his way across the bathroom and toward his chair parked in the hallway. The guinea pigs gave a round of squeaks like they felt the need to join in the chorus. Bangs and scrapes came next as Dad maneuvered his chair back into the living room.

He must have noticed the curtain was open this time once he entered the living room. He said, "What are ya doin'?"

"Watching."

"What for?"

I shrugged. "Janice watches every night."

"Janice is a crazy ol' coot. She probably waves and smiles at the damn thing while it does its trick or treating."

I turned to him. He was digging a cigarette from a pack. He leaned to the side of his chair and shut the oxygen tank off before placing the cigarette in his mouth. He used the arm of this recliner to pull himself to his feet before shuffling in a half circle and planting his ass in the recliner to watch TV. I let him light his smoke and take a puff before I spoke.

"Have you ever watched it?"

He didn't say anything for a long while, only stared at the tube, and I thought he might not have heard me. I was about to ask again when he responded.

Without turning from the television he said, "I never went out of my way but it made sure I knew it well the one time." He took another drag before he said solemnly, "I'd leave it alone if I were you. You'll end up like your mother."

I wanted to respond with something hateful and as mean as the blow he'd delivered. I was too young to remember how it'd happened. All I knew was it happened on the eve of Christmas . . . her favorite holiday. I could recall how sad she was the week leading up to the fateful event but I was too small to comprehend what was happening at the time and what the repercussions would be. From what I gathered as I grew older, she'd grown disheartened living in Strang. She'd begged and nagged Dad almost every day to pack up and leave. But he was nothing short of the most stubborn man in the world. Then one year All Hallows' Eve came and went in the usual fashion and he said something changed in her after the festival. She put up all the Christmas decorations the next day. The house and yard were filled to capacity with everything Christmas. As a kid I thought it was fantastic and I was probably a pestering little shit since the concept of time and adult emotions are lost on a child. She became distant and quiet. She stopped feeding Halloween. Dad had to keep up on the guinea pigs and put one out every evening. During the excitement of dinner and the ceremonial opening of one gift on Christmas Eve he forgot to feed Halloween. The best I could recollect was waking in the dark . . . and the screams. The sound of your parents screaming in fear for their lives isn't one you easily forget. Even all these years later.

I stared at the back of his head and said, "Sooner or later, on a long enough timeline, we'll all end up like Mom."

If he responded I didn't hear him and he didn't move. The electric current of fear creeping up my neck and scalp muted everything around me. The sensation was suddenly the only thing I could focus on. My heart began to hammer and my mouth abruptly went dry. I didn't want to turn around. I knew Halloween was out there. I knew it was out there and the curtain was open.

A part of me wanted to go directly to my room. I didn't want to turn around and acknowledge it. I wanted to pretend nothing was out of the ordinary and walk straight to the basement. I had no idea what I was thinking opening the curtain and trying to confront the damn thing like I had balls of steel. I didn't have the nerve to stare Halloween down. Dad was right. Janice wasn't fearless and hadn't grown complacent with Strang's plight. She was a lunatic. And I'd be a lunatic too if I tried to interact with Halloween or act as though it didn't bother me.

The sensation of dread and malice wasn't lessening any. It wasn't abating or intensifying. It was hovering and persistent. Halloween wasn't making its way down the street toward or away from the house. I knew deep down it wanted to screw with me and wouldn't be happy until it got what it wanted. I knew I had to either walk away or confront my fear of Halloween. I'd opened the curtain. I'd invited it to come face to face with me. I didn't hear the chuckle coming from it but felt it deep in my bones. It was like Halloween knew what I'd planned to do and now knew I was going to chicken out and had decided to stick around and fuck with me until I ran off to the basement without turning around. It reveled in knowing it would always win one way or another. I stared at the back of Dad's head and Halloween stared at the back of mine. I knew it. I could feel it. Its incessant whispering started but I couldn't understand what it said. It would torture me forever or until I died. Or until Dad died and I moved away. It tortured Mom. And I knew the process would go on and on and on until no one was left and Halloween knew no one had the guts to fight back. I knew there wasn't any way to win and I couldn't take it anymore.

I spun around before I could give it much more thought and came face to face with it. We were separated by a few inches and a flimsy pane of glass. And for the first time I thought maybe, just maybe, I'd gotten a glimpse of its true form. Its head was abnormally large and the eyes had no irises or pupils. The creature sat on its haunches so its head was level with mine. An orange light flickered deep within its chest, first on the right side and then the left. The light illuminated its ribcage and in the center of its chest was a black mass that could only be the beast's heart. The light flashes were erratic and mimicked the unpredictability of lightning. It lifted its lips in a sneer to expose long pointed teeth and tapped on the glass with a long nail.

Its lips moved in an unnatural manner as if mocking human speech, keeping its teeth exposed. It said, "Trick or treat, Barry."

Dad began coughing and wheezing. I couldn't breathe or move and I could've sworn my heart skipped a beat and my left arm began to tingle.

"Can I come inside?" it said.

I screamed. Dad screamed. Halloween laughed before it began shifting from one image to another. I swore it took the shape of my mother for the briefest second. The cage door on the step banged without the thing bending out of sight before the sharp yip of the guinea pig came. The glass of the door was painted with arterial blood as the thing laughed.

Dad and I screamed in unison although his sounded strangled and wet.

The creature sang the taunting song: "Trick or treat. Smell my feet. Give me something good to eat. Crackers, fruit will not do. Give me candy, I want two. Candy, candy I want four. Candy, candy I want more." The broken and bloodied body of the guinea pig hit the glass and cracked it.

I tried to jump back but tripped and fell on my ass. I kicked my feet and scuttled back away from the door and slammed my head into the curio cabinet. Dad made a rasping noise but I couldn't take my eyes off the blood-covered glass.

The thing laughed. "Sticky fingers. Tired feet. One last house. Trick or Treat."

Everything except the television went silent. I was afraid to breathe, waiting for whatever was to come next. But nothing happened.

I eventually turned to Dad. His face was frozen in a look of terror and he was gripping the front of his shirt. His skin was abnormally pale and his eyes were glued to the door. I waited a beat for him to regain himself but his expression didn't change.

"Dad?"

He didn't move. I simultaneously knew what happened and was in denial. I picked myself off the floor and went to him. I grabbed his forearm and gave it a shake before I accepted he was gone.

FIVE

I CALLED SHERIFF GRAYSON RIGHT AWAY and told him everything. He advised me not to disturb the body and told me to tell the county coroner I'd been asleep when he passed and I'd found him when I woke for work. The sheriff also informed me I'd be better off waiting until I could clean the front door as to not raise any suspicion from outsiders and told me he'd be over in the morning before hanging up.

There wasn't anything anyone could do until sunrise and only the people in Strang knew about Halloween. The whole secret was precarious at best. It seemed like there should be some people within the know. There was no way the townsfolk had never mentioned it to another soul outside town limits. Surely the residents had visitors stay overnight at some point. It was asinine to think no one had any family or friends they spoke to on the phone periodically. I tried to think of an instance when I'd noticed a stranger in town and couldn't recall anyone. If anyone had ever mentioned Halloween or what was happening here the outsiders were keeping it to themselves. It felt crucial for certain personnel from the county and neighboring towns to know. The county coroner, at the very least.

I wanted to do something for Dad, at least cover him up, but Grayson's words kept ringing in my mind to leave everything as it was. I ended up pacing nervously around the living room, feeling helpless. But every time I glimpsed the horrified expression on Dad's face I began to bawl uncontrollably.

Eventually I retreated to the basement to wait for morning. As hard as I tried, sleep never came. I lay in bed with the light on, staring at the wall, trying to process everything that happened. Dad was dead. I was alone. Those were the only two things bounding around in my skull. I couldn't think of much more beyond that. I didn't want to think about anything else because if I did I didn't know if I could live with the guilt of having caused his death. Seconds felt like hours and minutes felt like years as I waited for the sun to rise.

At the first rays of daylight I ascended the stairs. I collected a bottle of Windex, paper towels, and a plastic grocery sack from under the kitchen sink. I avoided looking at Dad as I slipped out the front door. The broken guinea pig lay in a bloody heap on the step. I placed the poor creature in the plastic sack before turning my attention to the dried and oxidized blood on the door.

As I was drying the door the church bell gave out a couple of weak gongs. The crows nesting in the bell tower squawked and took flight in the distance. The bell rang loud and clear for a couple of minutes before falling silent.

Janice stepped out her front door in a quilted housecoat, bleary-eyed, while the bell still chimed. She retrieved her cage without taking notice of me. A few minutes later a couple of the other residents on the street did the same as Sheriff Grayson's patrol car rounded the corner.

I was exhausted and numb. I stood on the step with the bag full of bloody towels and the dead guinea pig and stared at the cop car as it parked in front of the house.

Sheriff Grayson was a thin man twenty years my senior and it took him some time to exit his car. He stood by the driver's door of his cruiser and adjusted his trousers by pulling on the waistband. He assessed me with a frown before slowly making his way toward me. I noticed Janice's face pressed against her front window.

"Mornin', Barry," Grayson said. His voice was raspy and strained, as if he didn't speak often and when he did it was a chore.

"Mornin'."

"So what've we got?"

I was too exhausted to talk and pointed to the front door. The sheriff climbed the steps and I opened the door for him. I didn't think I could bring myself to follow him in the house but thought better of standing outside as the other neighbors tried to covertly spy on me while Janice stayed plastered to her front window, watching unabashedly.

There was an underlying smell of shit I hadn't noticed before when I entered the house. Normally I would've been embarrassed about it but I was certain the odor didn't have anything to do with our hygiene or the guinea pigs. Dad released his bowels in death.

Sherriff Grayson let out a low whistle as he stared at Dad. The guinea pigs responded to him. He circled the living room, taking a good look at the cages and the old family photos Mom hung decades ago, before stopping to inspect the front door. He ran his finger along the crack in the glass before turning to me.

"Ya provoked old Halloween, huh?" His eyes narrowed into a scornful expression.

"I didn't provoke it. I was watching it and . . ."

He harrumphed and let a beat of silence pass as if he were waiting for me to fess up to something more sinister. He finally said, "Well . . . I should hope not. I would've thought this house learned its lesson." He took in the living room walls again. "This town doesn't need two in one season."

I nodded in agreement, not wanting to think about the fall festival.

He grabbed his waistband and pulled his pants up half an inch. "I'll get on the horn to the county. Ya got everything covered?"

"Yes, sir."

"Stayin' in Strang?"

The question took me aback. It was the last thing from my mind at the moment.

"Uh, mm," I sputtered. "I was planning on—"

"There'll be paperwork to fill out. Funeral to plan. I would hope you'd tidy up ya daddy's affairs before hightailin' it outta here. Got an insurance policy to pay out?"

"Oh, uh, I don't know. Maybe?"

"See, thing is, most people are eager beavers to get the hell out of Strang once they can. I've seen it more times than I can count.

All their family is gone. Or the next to last ones got the dot." His frail voice grew stronger. "And they're done. They pack up and move in the middle of the night without givin' a lick about anyone but themselves. Leave their property taxes unpaid. Funeral expenses unpaid. End up leavin' the townsfolk involved high and dry. You get what I'm sayin', Barry?" He placed a hand on his hip by his holster.

I couldn't take my eyes off his gun when I nodded. When I redirected my gaze to his face he looked dubious and irritated with my nonverbal response.

I said, "I don't have any money to move."

"Doesn't stop most. 'Specially with the fall festival a hair's breadth away."

I wasn't sure how he wanted me to respond. Did he even want me to respond? Was he threatening me? I was too weary and exhausted to process whatever his intentions were. He continued to stare at me sternly and expectantly. I wanted to shout 'what the fuck do you want from me' and 'I'm too tired and my dad just died and I don't want to play your fucking mind games' but knew nothing good would come from it.

"I'm not going anywhere," I said. I wanted to add 'for now' but thought better of it. "Everything will get squared away. I promise." I'd say whatever it was he wanted me to say if it meant he'd hurry up and get Dad out of this house.

He pursed his lips before he said, "I'll be keepin' an eye out that ya do." He raised a bushy eyebrow, almost as in question. "I'll get on the horn to the coroner. Should probably let mister McCallister know ya won't be makin' it into work today."

"Yeah. I'll do that."

He didn't say anything else before he let himself out.

SIX

KATHY MANAGED TO COMBINE AN expression of shock and disgust when I entered the store on Thursday. "What are you doin' here? Your daddy died."

"Thanks for reminding me," I said.

I approached the checkout lane and retrieved my vest. Kathy stared at me openmouthed and I avoided making eye contact with her. I didn't think she was capable of compassion but if I had to deal with one more person looking at me with a sliver of pity I was going to snap. Why couldn't people leave a grieving person alone? I was tired of the half-whispered apologies and pitiful looks I'd gotten with every interaction since Dad died. All the 'sorry for your loss's didn't soften the blow. I'd never understood why people were inclined to murmur, mutter, and mumble their condolences as if speaking in a normal tone would break the griever's eardrums or wake the dead.

I didn't want to tell her why I was at work. It could possibly garner more pity. I didn't have a choice. Part of the reason I'd come to work was to occupy my mind. Left to my own devices I couldn't see anything other than the terrified and frozen expression Dad wore as the coroner removed him from the house. I couldn't scrub the image from my mind's eye no matter what I did. The other reason I was there staring at Kathy's sour face: after spending all day tearing the house apart, there was no sign of a will or insurance policy. Which meant if Sheriff Grayson was threatening me there was no way I'd be able to move out of Strang without at least paying for Dad's funeral costs. There was a possibility the sheriff was all talk but the threat of physical harm, or death, kept me from considering skipping town. I had a vision of him patrolling my house and the store constantly, waiting for me to bail, so he could use his itchy trigger finger. Besides, I didn't have any savings to leave town. And where would I go? It took all my meager check and Dad's lousy disability check to keep our household afloat. I had no idea what I was going to do without Dad's checks. I didn't think there was any way Mr. McCallister could afford to give me a raise or let me work extra hours. He wouldn't even forfeit a few measly dollars to purchase a new vest for me.

Kathy stared at me expectantly. "Well?"

"Well what?"

She appeared to be contemplating her next words and selected them carefully. "Don't ya have funeral arrangements to make?"

"Did it yesterday. It's not like there's much of a wait at the funeral home."

She opened her mouth to say something but stopped short. I knew there was no getting around what she wanted to know. She wanted the whole story. I'm sure her and the whole town received the basic information along with a few gruesome tidbits about how Dad went and possibly looked from the Sherriff. But what Grayson relayed to any of the townspeople about the incident wasn't directly from the horse's mouth. It wasn't full of the details of a one-on-one encounter with Halloween. Kathy wanted to feel privileged to be the first one to hear the whole story so she could call around town and recount it over and over to every gossipy resident who'd listen to her yammer on. I imagined her retelling the same tale: recalling how hangdog I appeared when I entered the store this morning, the conversation we were currently having, the recounting of Halloween's visit, all the way up to how I interacted with her or Mr. McCallister toward the end of the day. Not to mention how she would punctuate the whole story with a tirade about her opinion of me and the situation. And once she was done she would barely have disconnected the call before she was dialing the next person.

I sighed and already felt exhausted. The thought of talking to her made me want to take a nap. "Halloween showed up last night. He sort of did some things out of the ordinary."

It may have been the first time I'd ever seen Kathy look excited. "Like what?"

"He was menacing me through the window of the front door and it was more than what Dad's heart could take, apparently."

"Menacing? How?"

"I don't know if you want to hear the details. It's not for the faint of heart."

I wanted to smack myself in the forehead after the terrible and unintended pun. Kathy either didn't seem to notice or didn't care. Probably the latter.

She said, "I'm a big girl. Been here the whole fifty-four years of my life. Seen more get the dot than you. I'm sure I can stomach it."

"It uh . . . knew my name and asked to come in."

She almost jumped out of her chair as she yelled, "You fuckin' talked to it?!"

Mr. McCallister yelled, "Kathy! How many times"—he appeared in the doorway of the office with an angry expression—"do I have to—" He cut himself short once he spotted me and his features softened. "Oh, I didn't expect you back until Monday." He was at a loss to add anything else.

"Funeral isn't until tomorrow, sir. Trying to keep busy and occupy my mind."

"He was tellin' me what happened," Kathy said.

"Kathy," Mr. McCallister reprimanded her. "Leave the grieving man alone. Now's not the time to be rehashing what happened."

"It's okay," I said. "It's probably best if I get it off my chest."

Kathy pointed at me. She jabbed her finger at me repeatedly, causing the loose skin under her biceps to sway, while addressing Mr. MCallister. "He said it knew his name and invited itself in."

Mr. McCallister's eyebrows rose in shock. "You talked to Halloween?"

"I didn't instigate the conversation."

They both waited for me to elaborate.

"I watched for it and when it came to the door it said 'trick-or-treat' and addressed me before asking if it could come in."

Kathy said, aghast, "And you let it in?!"

"No. I'm not insane. It sung the trick-or-treat song before ..." I wasn't sure how descriptive I should get. "It killed one of our guinea pigs and sprayed blood all over before throwing it at our door and cracking the glass. Dad saw the whole thing and it was more than he could handle."

Mr. McCallister and Kathy looked at one another.

Mr. McCallister said, "Halloween has never tried to break in before. Well, I guess there was—" He stopped short. Realizing Halloween had broken into our home and took my mom years ago. "Not unless you don't give it a treat."

No one in the town referred to the animals as anything more than a treat. No one called them what they really were. A sacrifice. It was either the poor creatures or us. And it was easier to put a level of separation between the animals and us by referring to them as something that wasn't even living.

Kathy said, "Are you sure you didn't do anything to antagonize it? You know, your mama—"

"Kathy!" Mr. McCallister interrupted.

"The boy deserves to know his mama didn't act right before Halloween took her." She turned to me. "Your mama started messin' with that thing. Taunting it. Trying to reason with it. Said it was harassin' your family real bad."

I said, "I thought it was because Dad forgot to put out something for it."

Kathy shook her head. "She was tryin' to stop it. Remember?" she asked Mr. McCallister. "She'd come to the town meetings. Saying she'd talked to it and thought she could eventually convince it to stop. She said she was on to something. Thought she might figure out a way to make it go away."

The front door of the store opened and the bell rang as Sheriff Grayson entered. He stopped between the register and office, hooked his thumbs in his holster belt, and turned his head back and forth, observing the three of us. It was probably apparent by our guilty demeanor and expressions we were discussing Halloween and the incident.

Mr. McCallister spoke up, "Mornin', Sherriff. Is there anything I can help you find?"

"No no. Jus' here to speak with Barry 'bout the town meetin'." He took slow and deliberate steps toward me. "You comin' to the town meetin', Barry? I know it's tomorrow and your daddy's funeral is then but talked to Dooley and he said he'd have your service all done in time."

"Uh, I don't—wasn't planning after what's happened—"

"Doris sure could use your help for the fall festival," he said with a slight bit of enthusiasm. "Got rides this year." He smiled at Kathy before turning back to me. "Thinkin' if ya helped out we might be able to . . . compensate ya some of what we talked about yesterday."

"Uh, I guess I could help out then."

"That's what I like to hear. A community comin' together to partake in a happy and recreational activity." He stood up straight and adjusted his belt. He nodded at Kathy. "Y'all have a real nice day now."

He slowly strode to the door, observing everything as he passed it. He gave Mr. McCallister a half-hearted salute before exiting. We watched him through the windows as he strolled to his car parked at the curb. He stopped before opening the driver's door and waved at us. We all gave lazy waves in return.

Once he pulled away from the curb Kathy asked, "What was that all about?"

I said, "Pretty sure he's finding more ways to keep an eye on me."

SEVEN

THE TOWN MEETING WAS HELD in the gymnasium of the long abandoned school. The number of folding chairs set up was a bit ambitious but I was certain it was a reflection of how many residents used to live in Strang. Only about thirty seats were occupied when I entered. I took a chair toward the back on the outside aisle out of habit. Normally Dad would've parked his Jazzy Chair next to me on the occasions we attended.

A few of the attendees chatted amongst themselves. I noticed a lot of side-glances when I entered and the people talking to one another leaned closer and lowered their voices. I'd be a fool to think they weren't talking about what happened to Dad. I avoided making eye contact with any of them. I didn't want to give them the satisfaction of knowing their gossip bothered me.

Rhonda from the restaurant stood out like a sore thumb with her bright red hair. It was the first time I'd seen her at a council meeting I'd attended. She sat by herself toward the front and stared off in the middle distance with a sad expression.

The town council members sat behind the standard folding table. They were a motley crew of worn, aging, and dejected men and women. On the table in front of them was the dreaded stack of envelopes. The mayor, Doris, approached a podium situated to the side of the folding table. She was an elderly woman with a heavily lined face, sad eyes, and jowls that made her look more like a bull-dog than a human being.

Doris tapped the microphone. A few loud pops emanated from the speaker set in front of the podium. She leaned too close to the microphone and said, "Are we ready?"

Her voice was loud and distorted. A few people covered their ears as some squawks and squeals of feedback echoed through the gym. The treasurer rose from the table and made quick work of adjusting the volume on the lone speaker in front of the podium.

The mayor waited until he was finished before she continued. "As you all know, All Hallows' Eve is a week away. The town council has already made an itinerary of events that include some of the standard yearly staples. And this year we were able to budget two carnival rides." Her voice grew loud and excited when she announced the carnival rides and the speaker distorted her voice. "But before we get to that . . ." She turned to the council member. "Are there any requests or appeals since the last meeting?"

Old Hurly sat in the front row. He raised his hand and simultaneously yelled, "Yeah! Can we not have the fall festival this year?"

A ripple of chuckles emanated from the townspeople.

Doris sighed into the microphone and fixed her watery eyes on the crowd as a whole. "Anyone else?"

Another brave soul—a frumpy woman who I could never remember if her name was Eleanor or Elaine—raised her hand. The major pointed at her and insinuated she had the floor.

Eleanor or Elaine remained seated and said, "What's the point of carnival rides? There aren't any kids. It seems like a waste of town funds."

"Please save your questions for the end of the meeting," Doris chided her. She addressed the audience. "Does anyone have any requests or appeals?" She waited a beat before continuing. "If there is nothing more we can move on to our main objective. We need volunteers to help out with setting up and tearing down the festival." She retrieved a pair of reading glasses from the podium and placed them on the end of her nose as she lifted a paper to get a better view of the print. "We need someone with a pickup truck to run the hayride." She peered over her glasses at the gas station owner. "I take it Jacob will be so kind as to take care of this as usual."

"Yes, ma'am," he responded.

She made her way down the list. A handful of people volunteered to set up and tear down. Rhonda was one of a couple of women who volunteered to run the food and beer stand, which accounted for her presence. Old Hurly took the horseshoe competition mainly because he liked to harass the losers every year. And the town treasurer, Bill, was in charge of the costume-judging contest since there were only ever about a handful of people who actually made the effort to dress up. It wasn't like the fall festival was something any of us actually wanted to celebrate. It was foisted on us to boost morale and to preoccupy us before the night's awful conclusion. It was a sad gathering of middle-aged and elderly people trying to act like nothing was wrong with our town while, deep down, each of us feared the dot.

I was lost in thought and mentally numb since leaving Dad's funeral. I tried to focus on the festival and the meeting so I wouldn't break down into tears but I was finding this difficult. I found myself staring at the back of Rhonda's head, hoping she'd turn so I could catch a glimpse of her face.

A hand clamped down on my shoulder like a vice. I flinched and almost jumped out of my chair. The shock sent a bolt of pain through my chest. The person dug their bony fingers into my shoulder and kept me seated. I looked up and over my shoulder to see Sherriff Grayson giving me the stink eye.

Grayson bent to talk discretely to me. "I think that's you, boy. It's your last chance to volunteer."

"What?" I said.

Doris said, "It'll only be for two nights. We may ask the volunteer to do a few other small tasks but mainly we need someone who has a couple extra beds. Now you all know whoever does this has to keep things discrete. We can't have them running around after dark. Or telling outsiders what's goin' on here."

Elaine or Eleanor raised her hand. "What about the festival? Won't they find out when you announce the dot?"

Doris said, "We plan to play it off as a raffle of sorts."

Old Hurly said, "Might be kinda difficult if the person doesn't go quietly. Don't think anyone forgets how Timothy carried on."

Doris grew aggravated and almost shouted into the microphone. "It's not going to be a problem. We all know what's required of us. Anyone who would make a scene is a coward." She backed away from the microphone a few inches. "I think we all know the consequences of resisting. This is for the greater good." She turned to Elaine or Eleanor and answered her previous question. "We're doing this to boost morale and to take our minds off the task at hand."

A grumble ran through the crowd.

Grayson squeezed my shoulder again and shouted toward the front of the room. "Looks like Barry here is volunteerin'."

Everyone in the room turned toward me.

"You're willing to board the carnies?" Doris asked.

"Uh."

"Speak up," Grayson said and let go of my shoulder.

"Yeah . . . I, uh . . . I guess I have room." Rhonda gave me a sad smile from the front. "I could use the company." It took me a second to realize I'd said the last part aloud. In my mental fog I'd said what I wanted to say to Rhonda. I could feel my face flush.

"Good," Doris said. "Is there anything anyone would like to add?"

"Yeah," Old Hurly said. "Can we skip the fall festival *next* year?"

The mayor ignored him and said, "I need the volunteers to stay behind. Everyone else is free to go unless there are any further questions." She checked her wristwatch. No one spoke up and she banged the gavel, signaling the end of the meeting.

The people who did not volunteer moseyed toward the exit, picking up their hushed conversations they were ensconced in before the meeting. I ignored the sheriff and the side-glances and made my way toward the front to join the volunteers. Rhonda peeked over her shoulder at me but just as promptly turned her attention back to the group of volunteers huddling in the open space near the town council's table. The members were rising to stand near the others and my attention was drawn to the ominous stack of envelopes sitting deserted on the table.

The mayor began handing out a list of instructions to each person with locations and times to pick up or move the items needed for the event: tents, tables, bales of hay, etc. I stood at the back of the group and turned to look back at my seat to find Grayson slowly making his way toward the door. His eyes were glued on me as he went. I hadn't heard most of the directions given to the other people and only turned my attention back to the group when the mayor called my name. Everyone was staring at me.

"I'm sorry," I said.

"I need your full attention," Doris said.

I nodded and most of the group turned their attention to the papers they held and began reading through their assigned duties. Doris beckoned me with a wave of her hand and I made my way around the group. She held out a stack of papers to me. I spotted two rows of type on them, filling the first page. I took the papers and noticed the list of names of the townspeople. My heart leapt a beat as I realized what my job would entail. I'd never known who was in charge of the duty at hand and always imagined it was all on the shoulders of the mayor.

I opened my mouth to say something to Doris but she gave me a stern look and shook her head, indicating I wasn't to let the group know.

Doris said, "You'll meet me at nine in the morning the day before the event. I want you to give the carnies a hand with setting up the rides and fetching anything they might need. Try to have everything in order by five in the evening. Take them to an early supper at the diner and get them squirreled away before the sun sets." She inclined her head ever so slightly toward the envelopes and added, "In the meantime you can help out with setting up the town square in the evening. You can bring the other items with you when we meet the day before."

I kept my eyes on her and tried not stare at the table with an aghast expression. I nodded to convey I understood. I also understood she and I would be the last ones to leave the meeting to keep the horrible secret of who actual wrote every residents' name on the envelopes—sealing one unlucky person's fate—under wraps.

EIGHT

"HAVE YOU EVER WONDERED WHAT it does with them?" Jacob said.

We'd finally set the last bale of hay in the street. The bales doubled as a barricade and seating. Jacob and I were taking a short break, leaning against the tailgate of his truck and greedily drinking water. Both of us were taking the opportunity to observe Rhonda's hips shimmy as she wiped down a table.

I'd never given much thought about what Halloween did with the person unlucky enough to get the dot. I tried to recall a time when anyone mentioned the outcome and nothing came to mind. It didn't take a genius to figure out it murdered the person in question because they were never seen again. But what it did with them between the announcement and their demise wasn't something I wanted to think about.

"I don't know," I said. "I never really thought about it. I assumed it ... uh ... you know." I drew a finger across my neck. I waited a beat for him to respond and when he didn't I asked, "Why?"

Jacob shrugged his shoulders. "Lot of empty graves in the cemetery. Seems sort of weird. One would figure if it likes to torment us he'd bring the bodies back and do ... something horrible."

"But if it's eating them ..."

A horrified expression washed over his face. "That's ghoulish. Is that what you think it does?"

"That's what it does to the animals, doesn't it? Why wouldn't it do the same to us?"

"It could come into our houses any time it wants but it doesn't. If it wanted to eat us there's nothing stopping it."

"I thought that was the whole reason for the animals. Someone at some point had to have made an agreement with it to keep it from eating a townsperson every night. Right?"

He shrugged again. "I've never heard that."

"Because no one wants to talk about the boogeyman. You'd think the mere mention of Halloween would make the goddamned thing materialize out of thin air the way everyone tiptoes around the topic." I took another drink of my water. "What's your theory then?"

He frowned and contemplated for a moment. "Maybe it lets them go. Maybe it's all part of its tricks."

I suppressed a laugh. "Why would it do that?"

"Why does it do anything?"

I didn't have an answer for him.

After a beat he said, "Sometimes I wished I'd get the dot just to put an end to all of it."

The statement was asinine and I opened my mouth to respond but stopped myself. What did any of us have but this pathetic loop of despair until we keeled over or received the dot? The more I thought about it the more I sympathized with Jacob. Maybe it would be better to get the dot. At least it would be something. Maybe it would be oblivion. Maybe Halloween would make it quick so I wouldn't have to suffer through another year of this hell.

Old Hurly pulled a large piece of Astroturf toward the center of the street. At the end of the block I noticed the sheriff leaning against the wall of the police station. He appeared to be watching Jacob and me.

Jacob spotted Grayson. "Sheriff's got an eye on you. What did you do? Piss in his Cheerios? Seems like he's always waitin' for you to fuck up or something."

"Yeah."

Rhonda rounded the table and began wiping down a different area. Jacob and I got a nice view of her cleavage as she faced us. She looked up and spotted the two of us. My cheeks flushed and I diverted my eyes quickly. But before I could focus in on Old Hurly's bony ass sticking up in the air as he repositioned the Astroturf I thought I caught a glimpse of Rhonda smiling at me.

Jacob elbowed me in the ribs. "Neither one of ya are getting any younger. When are you two finally gonna hook up?"

"What are you talking about?" My face was on fire and knowing my embarrassment was on blatant display made me even more embarrassed. I was certain my face was the same color as Rhonda's hair.

Jacob chuckled before taking the last drink of his water. He shook his head.

I said, "I better help Hurly before he gives himself a heart attack." I threw my empty Styrofoam cup in the bed of his pickup before heading toward Old Hurly. I avoided making eye contact with Rhonda as I passed her.

NINE

THE PROCESS OF THE DOT was simple. An index card was inserted into a security envelope. There was one envelope for each townsperson. One index card would contain the dreaded dot. The mayor selected one resident to fashion the envelopes. Another person was assigned to randomly write the names of each resident on the envelopes. The town council would check to make sure all the residents' names were written on the envelopes and examine them for any tampering or doubles. The mayor and sheriff would then proceed to open the envelopes until they found the dot. And the person who was unfortunate enough to have their name written on the wrong envelope would become Halloween's sacrifice at the end of the fall festival.

I stared at the stack of envelopes on the kitchen table. The clock chimed in the living room. It was dusk and Halloween would be out on his nightly excursions now. I hadn't looked at the list or bothered to write the names on the envelopes and it needed to be done before tomorrow morning when I met with the mayor.

Each day, I went to work. After work I helped with setting up the square until it was nearing dark and we all had to go home. I would come home and clean another room in the house. I barely had time to eat and shower when the day was done.

The first day of cleaning was the most exhausting as I'd decided to drag Dad's soiled recliner and Jazzy Chair out to the garage. There was barely room with Dad's old Oldsmobile taking up most of the space. I couldn't remember the last time we'd actually driven the thing since everything in town was within walking distance (or rolling distance in Dad's case). A layer of grime coated the vehicle and two of the tires were flat. I decided to retrieve the keys and start the car, wondering how much Jacob would charge me to fix the tires. Maybe it was better to get in the car and drive as far away from Strang as possible. Who cared if I didn't have any money. I'd figure something out. But the car wouldn't turn over. And I didn't know a damn thing about cars. With each thing I found wrong with the car my hopes of ever leaving the town were crushed even further.

I gave up, put the car out of my mind, and resigned to cleaning the house the rest of the days.

Nothing much had changed in our home for as long as I could remember. Mom's room had never been touched and it took everything in me to pull the dusty sheets from her bed to wash them. The whole house smelled like a dirty ashtray because of Dad but I liked to think, beyond the cigarette smell and the dust, I could catch a small trace of Mom when I was in her room. It was faint and triggered vague childhood memories and I wasted an hour sitting on her bed and weeping once I got to her room.

But as draining as it was to deal with the wrongdoings of the past and forgotten memories and hopeful but crushed resolutions, it paled in comparison to the task of writing the names on the envelopes. One person, at my hand, would die in two days or disappear or succumb to whatever it was Halloween did with them. I'd left the burden of writing every name on the envelopes to the evening before meeting the mayor. It was dreadful enough to have been given the task but I wanted to live with the guilt for the least amount of time possible.

My hands trembled as I picked up the pages of names and shuffled through them. I noticed one name was crossed out with a black marker. But the letters could still be read and another layer of depression hit me like a ton of bricks. It was Dad's name.

I picked up the first envelope and held it up to the overhead light. Nothing could be seen through the security design printed on the inside of the envelope. And did I really want to be able to see the dot? Did I want that on my conscience? Knowing in advance who it would be?

I set the envelope on the table and carefully printed the first name on it before placing a checkmark beside the name on the list. I made sure to print neatly, as Mr. McCallister sometimes complained about my sloppy writing on the inventory log. My hands began to tremble after a dozen or so because I couldn't stop thinking about my part in all of it. The tremor reflected in my handwriting but the name was still legible. I tried to clear my head and think of anything else. I thought of Rhonda and the way her hips shimmied back and forth as she'd wiped down the counter of the food truck earlier in the afternoon.

As I set my pen on the next envelope, I heard it. The voice was low and menacing and I held my breath to make it out.

"Barry, Barry, quite contrary. How much does your life blow? With grim farewells and demons from hell and your mother screaming no, no, no!" It laughed.

The rattle of the cage came next. The guinea pig didn't make a noise. I sat with the pen poised to write, straining to hear anything else, for what felt like an eternity. Just at the moment I thought it had moved on to the next house a loud *thunk* on the window above the sink startled me and I almost jumped out of the chair. I turned to see a mixture of clear and yellow ooze with flecks of white splattered across the window, sliding slowly down the pane. Another egg hit the window before I realized what it was doing.

I didn't want to see it but the old man part of me was on my feet and to the window before I could think. Barely discernible in the scant light of the backyard and through the yolk-covered window, I spotted the blur of the ever-changing Halloween. It bellowed a raucous round of laughter once it spotted me.

Its movement was hard to comprehend but it appeared to be dancing a jig as it sang, "Five little pumpkins sitting on a gate. The first one said, 'Oh, my, it's late.' The second one said, 'There are witches in the air.' The third one said, 'But I don't care.' The fourth one said, 'Let's run, let's run!' The fifth one said, 'Isn't Halloween fun?'"

It made a sudden movement and another egg hit the window,

startling me. My heart leapt into my throat and I took a step back.

The thing grew still and growled the last bit of the song. "Then *woooo* went the wind. And out went the lights. Then one of the little pumpkins disappeared from sight."

It vanished in a flash but I could still hear its laughter in the distance.

I mumbled to myself, "Where did it get eggs?"

The incident did nothing to steady my nerves or my hand when I finally returned to the table to complete the envelopes.

TEN

AS SOON AS DAY BROKE I hooked up the garden hose and rinsed the egg debris from the kitchen window. Or at least tried to rinse the egg away. The goo had dried and was nearly impossible to clean with the hose. I had to retrieve a ladder from the garage and scrub the window with soapy water to remove the last bit of yolk.

The morning air was crisp. I pulled on a hooded sweatshirt before leaving the house to meet with Doris. The weight of the envelopes was much too light as I walked toward the town square. The plastic grocery sack I'd placed them in crinkled as is bounced off my leg with each step. A bag full of items meant to decide the fate of a single person felt as if it should weigh as much as a boulder. I know the guilt and anxiety weighing on my mind was as heavy, if not more.

A crow stood on the overgrown lawn of the church and eyed me curiously as I passed. As usual, there wasn't anyone about at this time.

I spotted the two large rides mounted on the back of two semis when I rounded the corner toward the barricaded square. They were parked on the street next to the barrier Jacob and I had built from bales of straw. One truck was filled with rounded carts and everything was painted red and blue. The other was purple and green and a sign peeked out of the jumble reading 'Alien Abduction'.

A group of people milled around a weathered van. I'd never seen any of the people or the vehicle before. Doris stood to one side, paying no attention to the group of people. She spotted me and kept her eyes locked on me as I approached.

The group looked worn down and harried. A lot of them wore rumpled clothing and appeared as though they hadn't bathed in a while. Most of them ignored me as I neared but a few eyed me dubiously.

I stopped in front of Doris and handed her the bag. She took it.

"All done?" she asked.

I nodded. Her face was unreadable. It seemed like such a task, whether you have any direct involvement in it or not, would make you feel something. But she took the bag as nonchalantly as if she were taking a bag of groceries. There was no enjoyment or resentment in buying groceries. There was only the feeling of having to deal with it as sustenance to keep one alive. The heartlessness of it all made my stomach churn. The duty of All Hallows' Eve was as banal as any household chore to the people of Strang.

Doris turned to the others. "Okay, folks," she said. "This here is Barry. He's going to give you a hand and he has been generous enough to give up a couple of rooms in his house."

I whispered to her, "I thought there was only two."

"There are," she responded. "It takes more than three people to set up the rides. The extras will be heading back to Millville to stay at the motel. You'll be hosting the two ride operators, Addisyn and Henry." She craned her head to look over the crowd, trying to spot something. "Henry," she called, "where's Addisyn?"

An overweight man with greasy long hair, wearing an extremely worn hair metal band shirt said, "Don't know. Think she went to her truck." When he spoke I noticed he only had half his teeth.

The door of the semi housing the Alien Abduction ride opened. A tanned and hardened woman exited the truck. Her thin hair was feathered in a style I hadn't seen in a decade or two and its color was indeterminable. It could've been dirty blond or light brown or possibly red. It was hard to tell by the state of her hygiene. She wore acid washed jeans with a sleeveless flannel shirt, topped with a jean jacket, its sleeves having met the same fate as the flannel shirt. Her boots clopped on the asphalt as she approached Doris. Her mannerisms were not graceful.

The woman stopped by Doris and jerked her head back to clear the hair from her face. She said, "This the fella we're housing with?"

"Yes," Doris said. "Addisyn, this is Barry."

"Nice to meet ya." Addisyn extended her hand for a shake.

I took her hand gingerly and she took ahold of the situation by squeezing my hand so hard I thought it might break. Her eyes were so dark brown they appeared black, which made her stare intense and unnerving. She gave my hand one firm pump before slipping both her hands into the back pockets of her jeans and striking a casual pose. Her eyes darted around at the buildings in the town square. The word 'predator' came to mind as I observed her.

Henry approached us and introduced himself. He struck me as simple but knew everything there was to know about the rides and their setup. He began rambling immediately about what needed to be done in great detail.

Doris was the one to save all of us the lecture. "I'm sure this is something you can go over with Barry once you all start." She lifted her wrist as if she was looking at the time but I noticed she wasn't wearing a watch and I wondered if the other two noticed. "There isn't a whole lot of daylight around here and it looks like you have a lot to do before dinner time. I'm sure the rest of your crew would like to get to their motel before nightfall as well."

"Sure, sure," Henry said. "We'll get right to it."

I noticed movement in the window of the diner. Rhonda was observing the group. Old Hurly stood next to her. I looked around to the other businesses on the street and noticed someone watching us from the window or doorway of each one.

"Right," Doris said. She handed Henry a thick envelope. "Half up front. Half at the end."

"We appreciate your business," Henry said. He took the envelope and tucked it into the pocket of his greasy jeans.

Doris only nodded at him before turning from us and heading down the street. Once Doris was far enough away she couldn't hear, Addisyn slapped me on the shoulder.

"Looks like you're our bitch for the next forty-eight hours," Addisyn said.

Henry laughed.

"Guess so," I said.

They directed me toward the group to get started.

ELEVEN

I WASN'T USED TO THE type of physical labor the carnies put me through. I wasn't in the greatest shape, and at first glance of the carnival workers, you would think they were worse off than I. But after learning their terms—that they were paid the same no matter how long it took—I understood the feverish burst of energy they had as soon as Doris was on her way.

Henry barked orders and the crew began unloading the rides from the semi, climbing to the top and tossing large pieces down as if they were nothing. I was fearful of having something fall on my head and brain me so I stood back and waited until another person handed me something and told me where to go with it.

A wiry old guy with no teeth, named Pete, put it into perspective for me. He said, "It's best to get it done as quickly as possible. Time is money. I'd rather get paid a hundred dollars an hour instead of ten. And still have time to jerk off." He also gave me the sage advice to 'never shit on my own time'. Meaning I should wait until I was clocked in to my day job to defecate so I would get paid to do it.

After twenty minutes I was winded and my chest was tight. I placed my hands on my knees to catch my breath, and once I'd re-gained myself, Addisyn made it clear by her glare I was more hin-drance than help. Henry politely told me to take a seat at a picnic table set up for the food truck and rest. I took the instructions for what they really were: get the hell out of the way and let us do our job. I wasn't about to argue with them. Moving a few boxes of canned goods was the extent of my daily physical activities. A far cry from slinging around hundreds of pounds of steel.

I took to watching Addisyn's every move. The muscles in her arms flexed impressively as she hauled a large part of the Tilt-A-Whirl from the truck to the setup location. Between carrying parts her eyes would dart around to the businesses and up and down the street. The head flick to clear the hair from her face appeared to be a tick of some sort or another. Every so often she would light a cigarette and it stayed in the crook of her mouth as she carried items. She squinted one eye against the smoke as she worked. Her expression was stern until she noticed me watching. She gave me a forced smile and the expression was more menacing than warm. I could feel my face reddening when I was caught watching her. There was something wolfish about her. As if she was observing the area to find her prey. It made me feel vulnerable for some reason, as if I was the prey she was hunting for.

The crew was fast, completing and testing the setup by four in the afternoon. They gathered around the van as Henry counted through the cash Doris handed him earlier. Once the funds were dispensed the extra people not staying with me crowded into the van and left for Millville.

The three of us stood in the middle of the street. I observed the impressive rides they'd constructed and they inspected the businesses and other activities for the festival around us.

Addisyn spoke first. "What's there to do 'round here? This place seems real dead."

Henry watched me expectantly. I had a hard time looking directly at Addisyn. Her eyes were so intense.

I rubbed the back of my neck nervously. "Well, I could take you guys to get dinner."

"I could eat," Henry said. He rubbed his bulging belly.

"You can always eat," Addisyn snapped at him. She turned to me. "Where's the waterin' hole?"

"Uh," I said. I pointed down the street toward the lone bar.

"That's a start," she said. She started toward the bar.

"Actually," I called after her. "They'll be closing in a couple of hours. And so will the diner. If you're hungry it's best to eat first."

She stopped and looked at her watch. "What kinda bar closes at six?"

I shrugged.

Henry looked at me with a dubious expression. "You sure they close at six or are ya pullin' our legs? Ya wouldn't be one of those holy rollers lookin' down on folks wantin' a drink every now and then?"

I shook my head. "No, sir. It's just . . ." I hadn't given a lot of thought to what I was going to tell these people about the curfew. I'd had a few ideas but they were all too ridiculous. "Strang has a curfew." I would have to come up with something quick.

Addisyn rejoined us. "Curfew? Fur what?"

"Uh, well . . ."

Both of their attention focused on something to my right. Light footfalls sounded from behind me, and before I had a chance to turn, Sherriff Grayson stood beside me.

"Bears," Grayson said.

"Bears?" Henry and Addisyn said in unison.

The explanation was so outlandish I almost joined the two in their questioning.

"They've been runnin' amok after sundown," Grayson said. "Knockin' over trashcans. Terrifyin' the townsfolk." He leaned in toward the two and lowered his voice. "Been eatin' up the pet population."

"Really," Henry said more as a statement than a question.

"Helluva mess," he responded. "Been trying to catch the bugger for quite some time now. His head would make one heck of a trophy down at the station."

Addisyn said, "Wouldn't of thought bears would be in such a flat and treeless place." Her tone and squint-eyed expression conveyed her skepticism.

Grayson scrutinized her quietly for a few seconds. The air between them grew uncomfortable and there appeared to be a silent battle of the wills passing between the two.

"Coyotes," Grayson said a tad too loud, "were indigenous to the plains and southwest but somehow they've made their way all the way up to Niagara Falls. Won't be long before they make it to the east coast. Sometimes Mother Nature doesn't play by the rules."

I thought Grayson might have been better off telling them there were coyotes on the prowl versus bears. There really were coyotes in our area. They were rare but they'd been spotted every now and then. And a coyote could be the cause of all the delinquencies he'd named off. But I guess a bear sounded more menacing. I know I would be more reluctant to be out after dark if I knew there was a bear in the area than a coyote. Coyotes were skittish. Bears were more likely to attack.

"Guess so," Henry said.

Grayson nodded at him. "Well," he said, "I ought to let you folks get back to your business." He looked up at the sky. "Not much daylight to be had this late in the season. Y'all have a good one." He made sure to give me a stern look before heading for the police station.

Once he was out of earshot, Addisyn said, "What an asshole." She flipped her head to clear the hair from her face.

I suppressed a laugh but Henry let loose a series of bellows. There was a slight hesitation in Grayson's stride as he approached the station but he refused to acknowledge us as he entered. He probably thought the laughter was about him and he'd be right.

Addisyn pulled a trucker's hat I hadn't noticed before from the back pocket of her jeans and put it on her head. "Please tell me there's a grocery store or a gas station where I can acquire some beer and cigarettes."

I nodded and pointed toward the gas station. "Jacob has some. Don't think it'll be anything too fancy. Not much of a selection. Same with the grocery store."

"Don't matter," she said. "As long as they get the job done."

"How 'bout some grub first?" Henry said.

"I'm not much of a cook," I said. "I planned on taking you to the diner. They have an okay selection. We should probably eat soon if we want to make it back to my place before sundown. We'll stop at the gas station before heading back to my place."

They agreed and I led them to the diner. Old Hurly was stationed in his normal spot with a cup of coffee and a newspaper when we entered. A couple other people were sitting at the counter. Rhonda appeared from the kitchen when we entered and she was already retrieving three menus as I directed the two toward a booth by the window. The two carnies sat on one side, Addisyn taking the side closest to the window, Henry taking the aisle. I sat opposite them. Addisyn stared intently out the window.

Rhonda was at our table before we'd even gotten settled. She sat menus in front of each of us. I tried not to stare at her cleavage as she bent forward to place a menu in front of Addisyn. Henry made no attempt to divert his gaze. She pulled a pad of paper from a pocket in her apron. "Can I get y'all some drinks to start?" Rhonda asked.

We placed our drink orders, which were a hodgepodge of water, coffee, and soda before Rhonda disappeared. The other two scanned the menus. I already knew what I wanted and didn't bother. Addisyn must have made up her mind quickly as she closed her menu and sat it in the middle of the table.

She placed her elbows on the table. "Where is everyone?"

I didn't have to look at the others in the diner to know they were listening in on our conversation. Even if I turned to observe them they wouldn't have made the slightest move indicating they were doing anything other than casually enjoying their meals. I wasn't a good impromptu bullshitter. I hated that I'd been put in charge of lying to these people. *Anyone* else in town would've been a better fit to do this. Now I knew why Grayson was so determined to get me to do it. He wanted me to slip up somehow or another.

I decided to play stupid. "What do you mean?"

Henry kept scanning his menu and said, "Ain't no one around is what she means. Other than nosy nellies peekin' out the windows up and down the street we haven't seen much of anyone." He looked up from the menu at me as if he would wait for a response from me before continuing his quest to find a dinner that would quench his appetite.

"The road is blocked off." I couldn't believe I'd come up with a reasonable answer on the fly. "People are probably resting up for tomorrow's festivities."

"It all seems strange, if ya ask me," Addisyn said.

"Well, um . . ."

Henry interjected. "The town *is* strange minus the 'e.' Get it? Strang."

She gave him an annoyed look. He ignored her and scanned the menu again. Rhonda appeared with our drinks.

Rhonda asked, "Know whatcha want yet? Or do you need a few more minutes?"

"I'll have the pork fried steak," Henry said.

"Same," Addisyn said.

Rhonda turned to me. "The usual?"

I could feel my face grow hot. I nodded and noticed Addisyn smirking at me. Rhonda collected the menus and headed toward the kitchen. Henry tried to slyly watch Rhonda's rear end as she walked away but was doing a poor job of hiding it.

"Boy, you got it bad," Addisyn said. "Don'tcha?"

My face grew even hotter and I could feel a layer of sweat forming on my face. "Got what bad?"

"You're a terrible lair," she said. "Plain as day you got it bad for that redhead."

Henry clasped his hands together and leaned toward me. He spoke barely above a whisper. "Plain as day somethin' weird goin' on here. Ain't no kids that I've seen. And the kiddies are the nosiest of all. Every place we go there'll be a few of 'em spyin' on us as we set up. Not here. Don't make sense for a town this small to pay for carnival rides. Something smells fishy to me."

Old Hurly coughed as if he'd heard every word and was warning me to keep my mouth shut. I side-glanced over to the old man and the other patrons before meeting the eyes of the two carnies.

"The mayor . . ." I said. "The town council thought it would be a good . . . for a change in the fall festival events. To mix things up."

Henry sat back and observed me for a moment. I could feel a nervous sweat breaking out all over my body. I rubbed my sweaty palms on my pants.

Addisyn smacked Henry's arm. She said, "Give the guy a break. He's jus' doin' what he's told." She gave him a stern look and the two appeared to have some sort of wordless exchange.

Henry held up his hands in a defensive manner. "'Ight. None of my business. Long as I get paid. What do I care 'bout this shithole town?"

Rhonda approached our table. She balanced one plate in the crook of one arm while holding the other two in each hand. She placed each plate in front of us and retrieved sets of utensils wrapped in napkins from her apron and distributed them to each of us. She inquired if any of us needed anything additional before retreating again.

Addisyn stared out the window as Henry and I ate in silence. Eventually she turned to her plate and spoke to no one in particular. "I'm definitely gonna need some beer."

TWELVE

ADDISYN HELD A SMOKING CIGARETTE between her lips while she and Henry each carried two cases of cheap beer on the walk home. She still managed to flick her head every so often to clear the hair from her face. I wasn't sure how she managed to do so with a lit cigarette in her mouth and not singe her hair or get ashes in her eyes but I was certain it was an acquired skill she'd learned over the years.

I noticed small movements in the curtains of the occupied houses as we passed them and knew everyone in town was curious about the temporary newcomers. They were also eager for us to pass so they could place their cages out for the night. The sun was setting and I kept glancing at my wristwatch nervously. We had ten more minutes before the sun would slip over the horizon and half a block to go. Plenty of time but, nevertheless, it made me antsy. It would put anyone living in Strang on edge. By now on most days everyone would be in their houses and ready to go. I still had to covertly put my cage out without the carnies seeing me and asking questions.

Addisyn spoke around her cigarette. "Sure are nervous 'bout that curfew."

"Uh, yeah," I replied.

Henry said, "Everyone 'round here seems really jumpy."

"Well, I, uh . . ."

"Y'all get a ticket or somethin' for not bein' in on time?" he asked.

Genius. Henry came up with the perfect answer for me. "Yeah. It's the dumbest thing. The sheriff is a real stickler about it. I don't want to get hit with a hundred-dollar ticket. And I'd hate for you guys to get stuck with one too."

"That guy acts like he's got a stick up his ass. I'd jus' throw it away anyhow," Addisyn said.

She spat the lit cigarette on the sidewalk and it fell onto a patch of dried leaves. I stamped on it to make sure it was out and wouldn't start the leaves on fire. That was the last thing Strang needed. I didn't even want to think about people fleeing from their houses after nightfall with Halloween on the loose. Or what the carnies would think as a house burned to the ground and everyone watched from their windows, not helping, and no fire department arriving to put out the flames, and everyone hoping the fire didn't spread to the next house before the sun came up.

We arrived at the house without another word. I quickly ushered the two inside. I led them to the Frigidaire. They began opening the cartons of beer and loading them into the nearly empty icebox. I took the time to slip back into the living room.

I checked my watch and noted I had less than six minutes. Without ceremony or compassion I opened a cage, grabbed a guinea pig, placed it in the outdoor cage. I didn't even give the poor thing any hay. As noiselessly as I could, I opened the door and placed the cage on the step. Janice was leaning out her door, wearing a quilted house coat and slippers. She'd just placed her cage down when she spotted me. She smiled beatifically at me and waved. I noticed the few other neighbors on the street hurriedly performing their nightly ceremony, tomorrow night being the only night of the year they wouldn't have to place the sacrifices on their step. It was the only night of the year when everyone, with the exception of one, was allowed to be out after dark with no repercussions. I waved hurriedly at Janice before shutting the door.

I began pulling all the curtains shut in the living area.

Addisyn entered the living room holding an open can of beer. She said, "Worried the bear will see ya?" She gave me a dubious and knowing grin before taking a long drink of her beer.

"Uh, no. Just nosey neighbors. It's a little irritating, everyone wanting to know your business."

Henry appeared behind her holding his own can of booze. "Where's the pisser?"

I pointed down the hall. "First door on your left."

He slipped down the hallway with his beer. Addisyn spotted Dad's ashtray and stared at it longingly.

I said, "It's okay to smoke in here."

She was pulling the pack of cigarettes from her shirt pocket before I'd finished the sentence. She would've lit up anyway. She coughed once without covering her mouth before placing the cigarette between her lips and lighting it. The sound of the toilet flushing came from down the hall and the door opened immediately. I thought, *Henry doesn't wash his hands after holding his member.* He rejoined us in the living room. Addisyn began looking around at the photographs.

"I guess I should show you your rooms," I said.

I led them down the hallway and turned the light on in Dad's old room. I told Henry, "This is where you'll be sleeping." They both followed me to Mom's room. The room was dark but the curtains were open.

In the dim twilight outside I spotted the blur of Halloween standing in the side yard, staring at me. For the briefest moment I spotted the orange flashes of light emanating from its chest. My heart stuttered and a sharp pain shot through my ribcage and into my back. I bit back a yelp. I don't know which would've caused me to cry out more, the pain in my chest or shock of spotting Halloween when I was supposed to be hiding it from the carnies. I tried to act casual. I flipped on the light and crossed the room and pulled the curtains closed. A cold and clammy sweat pricked my skin instantly. My face flushed hot as I turned back to the two.

The cards were stacked against me. I was a terrible liar and Halloween made it its personal goal to screw with me every night. There was no way I was going to be able to keep it under wraps and a secret from Addisyn and Henry. I was destined to fail. And where exactly was that going to leave me? Indebted to Grayson? A slave to Strang? Dead?

Addisyn said, "You don't have to close the curtains."

I said the first thing I could think of and was afraid I was going to sound like a skipping record. "Nosey neighbors."

She shrugged and entered the room. Henry looked at the odds and ends on Mom's dresser and Addisyn headed straight for the closet. I was about to protest when she opened the door to expose a small hoard of Mom's Christmas decorations and her few remaining clothes on hangers. Addisyn took a swig of beer before placing the cigarette with an impossible amount of ash clinging onto the end in her mouth so she could shove the clothes on the hangers to the side.

When she spoke the ashes fell on the floor. "What's all this?" She either didn't notice she'd ashed on the floor or didn't care.

Henry began riffling through Mom's stuff on the dresser. I staunched the desire to yell at them both about how rude it was to screw with other people's things. The two were worse than a couple of kids. Their prying amped my anxiety to a new level I didn't know existed.

"My mom was really into Christmas," I said.

Henry lifted a snow globe with an entrapped Santa and his sleigh from the dresser. He shook it. "Guess so," he mumbled before shoving it in Addisyn's direction for her to observe.

She watched the tiny pieces of plastic swirling within the globe, uninterested. She and Henry took a long drink of their beer at the same time. I thought, *I could really use a beer myself if the two were going to keep me on tiptoes all night.*

I said, "You should see the attic. Hey, you guys wouldn't mind if I took one of your beers, would ya?"

"Help yourself," Henry said. "Got plenty to go 'round."

"Where's the attic?" Addisyn asked.

THIRTEEN

AFTER THE THIRD BEER I was slaphappy enough that not only did I not care the two carnies were perusing through Mom's things, I was leading them through the stuff and giving them any backstory I could recall from each item. We found ourselves in the chilly attic, opening boxes under the sickly glow of the single exposed bulb and strands of multicolored Christmas lights.

Henry sat on a cardboard box stuffed with green garland. His weight buckled the box and made it look like a demented beanbag chair. He was surrounded by empty cans of beer and wearing a moth-eaten Santa hat. He laughed at us as Addisyn and I stumbled around the small dusty place decorating a long abandoned artificial tree from my childhood. Addisyn found one of Mom's long forgotten Christmas sweaters, and even though it was several sizes too small for her, she'd still managed to pull it over her shirt. After lifting her arms to place an angel on the top of the tree, the sweater managed to ride up over her belly and she hadn't bothered to pull it back down.

The tree was only half decorated when the lights and the alcohol I rarely consumed began to make my head swim. I found a box of my own to sit on and pulled it over by Henry before flopping down on it so hard the lid buckled. The sound of breaking glass followed, sending the other two into a fit of hysterics. I was probably lucky nothing inside penetrated the cardboard and sliced into my buttocks.

Once they'd settled down Addisyn abandoned the tree too, slammed back the last bit of beer in her can, and belched loudly before crushing the can. Somewhere in the distance an animal made a horrible and shrill scream.

"What da fuck was that?" Henry said and laughed again.

Addisyn stooped to retrieve a beer from the carton we'd brought with us to the attic. She waved her fingers at him and in a spooky voice said, "Fuckin' chupacabra."

Henry laughed heartily and I couldn't help but join him. If they only knew, they probably wouldn't think it was so funny.

Addisyn looked at me as she opened another beer. "Place is fuckin' weird. Like . . . bad weird. Gives me the heebie-jeebies."

The alcohol must have tamped my ability to mask my inner thoughts—something I wasn't good at in the first place—as both their expressions morphed into concern. Or maybe I wasn't seeing them through a sober eye. Either way, I could see they were expecting me to elaborate in some form or another.

Henry said, "Why is this place so weird? It's like that movie." He snapped his fingers as he tried to recall the name. "Oh, damn. You know . . . it's the one where everyone is in a cult and the woman is havin' a baby—"

"*The Stepford Wives*," Addisyn offered.

"No. No. They havin' a devil baby and there's all these old people—"

"*Rosemary's Baby?*" I asked.

He snapped his fingers and pointed at me. "That's the one!"

"'Cept ain't no babies," Addisyn added and took a healthy swallow of beer. She eyed me carefully.

Several things spun through my muddied thoughts. I was well aware, in my inebriated state, of my appointed job while housing the two. I may not have been a daily drinker but I could handle myself without being an asshole after a few beers. And I wasn't one to break down and water my beers with tears. I was a merry drunk. But there was one negative side to me once I'd reached a certain state of drunkenness and it included unbridled and brutal honesty. It was the reason I didn't drink all that often while Dad was alive.

The couple of New Years' Dad and I chose to have a few drinks to ring in the new year in front of the television turned into an airing of grievances/pity party. I would complain about all the things he did that got under my skin and he would go on and on about how the world hated him. After a few years we stopped the tradition. I resigned to bottling up my feelings and Dad was pretty good at throwing a pity party every day without the added cost of alcohol. I was overly aware in those few seconds of awkward silence passing between the three of us of the threats from Grayson. The rules of Strang had been tattooed into my brain my entire life and never telling outsiders about Halloween was at the forefront of my mind even with the beer fuzzing my thoughts. But with the added stress of being responsible for someone's demise tomorrow and being the one person with the burden of hosting the two outsiders and the weight of grief over Dad's recent departure and how Halloween had taken a great interest in screwing with me more than any other resident in Strang, the dam holding my mouth shut ruptured.

I told them everything. Neither of them said anything or interrupted me as I let it all out but their faces went through several changes of emotions and switched back and forth from skepticism and belief and shock. I wasn't sure how much time passed since I began and the two stared at me dumbfounded once I'd finished. I let the silence sink in for a few seconds as they struggled to process what I'd told them.

I said, "You think I'm crazy."

Henry sputtered a few times, tying to come up with an appropriate response.

"No, no," Addisyn said. "It's jus' a lot to take in." She chugged the last of her beer and I wasn't sure if she needed the drink to process the outlandish story or if she was stalling in order to come up with something appropriate to say to the insane person claiming there was some supernatural entity roaming the town as we spoke, gobbling up all the critters the residents left out for it.

"It's true," I said. "You guys said so yourselves. The town is weird. That's why." I shot to my feet and got lightheaded. I was never sure why anyone past their twenties would ever do drugs or drink when they could just stand up quickly. I grabbed a support beam above my head and waited for the dizziness to pass. Once I'd regained myself I said, "Come on. I'll show you if you don't believe me."

Addisyn flipped the hair out of her face. "Y'on't have ta do that."

Henry stood and swayed. "Ya mean you can show it to us? Right now?"

"I can try," I said. "It seems to be pissed at me and has been going out of its way to screw with me."

"I wanna see," Henry said. He started toward the dropdown ladder.

"Henry," Addisyn chided him.

"Be careful," I said, indicating the descent. I followed him.

Addisyn made a disgruntled noise but grabbed the cooler and started dragging it toward the opening in the floor. Henry started down the stairs first. He dropped to his knees and carefully backed down the rickety stairs cautiously. I followed his method and Addisyn handed down the cooler of beer before she did the same.

We made our way to the living room and I threw open the curtains facing the street. The three of us stood there staring out the window. The other two watched skeptically as nothing happened.

Henry popped open another can of beer. "How long's this gonna take? 'Cause I gotta take a leak."

I flipped the locks to the window and almost fell as I pulled it open. The windows were as old as the house and ran on a rope and pulley system. But neither Mom nor Dad had been much for allowing fresh air in. No one in Strang was, lest they forget to shut a window after sundown. I managed to crack the window a couple of inches and dropped to my knees in front of it. My knee cracked loudly and there was a pain dulled by the alcohol and I silently hoped I hadn't done something that would hurt tomorrow when I woke. I put my mouth to the cracked window and yelled, "Hey! Halloween! Hey, asshole! Got some people here who want to see you!"

I grabbed the sill and hoisted myself to my feet. The old wood of the sill cracked and pulled away from the wall and I fell on my arse. Addisyn gasped and stumbled back a few steps. It took me a second to realize Halloween was standing right outside the window. It was a dark blur under the streetlights outside. Its darkened shadow was darker than even the darkest night. As if it were made up of a black hole.

Henry wheezed and sputtered and a pattering sound came from behind me. I scuttled backward, sobering almost instantly, until I put my hand in something wet.

"What the fuck?" Addisyn said, backing away until she bumped into an end table.

The guinea pigs began to squeal shrilly.

Halloween solidified into the thing it'd become the night Dad died. The darkened part of its chest was a black hole. It bent forward, placed its exceptionally long fingers through the window, and grabbed the sill. Halloween lowered its head to the crack and began to recite a rhyme.

"The moon shines on a frightful scene. Ghouls and goblins to make you scream. Jack-o'-lanterns with eerie light, to illuminate the darkest night. In the witching hour banshees wail. Black cats lash their bushy tails. Reverse the number in thirteen. And then you'll know it's Halloween." The thing laughed. "Aren't you going to invite me in, Barry? It looks like you've started the festivities early."

It pulled its head away from the crack and slowly reversed its fingers to curl around the bottom of the window. The window shuttered and jumped a half inch in the track as Halloween began to open it.

Addisyn shrieked and bolted from her position. She grabbed the top part of the window and threw all her weight into slamming it shut. A small crack appeared in the pane when it banged back in place. And from my position on the floor I barely perceived Halloween retracting its fingers right before the window came down on them. It put its face close to the glass directly in front of Addisyn's face. She backed away and I scrambled on my hands and knees to the window. Beyond the oppressing figure of Halloween I spotted Janice standing in her window, watching. I didn't have time to think about the ramifications of her observing Halloween screwing with me while I was hosting the carnies. Or the fact she most likely spotted Addisyn confronting Halloween. Or how she could possibly pick up her telephone and call any one person in the whole town and by morning everyone in Strang, including Grayson, would know the carnies knew our secret. I snatched the edges of the curtains and pulled them closed.

"Holy fuck!" Addisyn shouted.

Halloween laughed outside. The laughter grew softer and softer as it moved down the street, echoing off the houses as it moved.

I got to my feet and turned to face the other two. Both were pale as a sheet. The front of Henry's pants was darkened and it dawned on me what the wet thing was my hand had touched. I held my hand up and away from me. A grimace crossed my face.

Henry said, "I done pissed myself."

FOURTEEN

THE VISIT FROM HALLOWEEN SOBERED the three of us.
Addisyn and Henry were keyed up like children on Christmas.
We had to launder Henry's pants and the time spent doing so was
filled with the questions no one had ever been able to answer: How
long has it been here? Has anyone tried to kill it? Why doesn't everyone leave?

We spent the rest of the night sitting around the kitchen table.
I'd carried my record player up from the basement to play music
softly as we spoke. We tried to regain our beer buzzes while I answered—or not answered, depending on how you looked at it—their
questions. Around three in the morning I realized I could drink until the cows came home and wouldn't get drunk. The drinking was
making me tired and I was certain I wasn't going to feel so hot when
I woke up. I tried to wrap the conversation up by making the two
agree they weren't allowed to ever talk about Halloween to anyone
once they left Strang and to pretend like everything was normal
tomorrow. But the two weren't completely ready for bed.

"Y'all are really gonna sacrifice someone tomorrow?" Henry
asked. "Jus' doesn't seem right. Ya don't even act like it bothers ya."

I added another empty beer can to the ever-growing pyramid on
the table. I yawned and said, "At some point you just resign. There
isn't anything we can do."

"But," Addisyn interjected. "It hasta have a weakness. Isn't there anythin' that bothers it? Like a kryptonite for Superman?"

"I'd like to think if we knew, we would've gotten rid of the thing a long time ago," I said.

Addisyn lit another cigarette. At the rate she was going she'd be out before the sun came up. She blew smoke above her head while staring at the kitchen table. She set her elbow on the table and rubbed her temple with the thumb of her cigarette-holding hand. Without looking up, she said, "Nothin' never happened to aggravate it." She said it as a statement and not a question.

"Well," I said, "my mom pissed it off."

"Whatcha mama do?" Henry said.

I looked at him and gave a small laugh before pointing at the Santa hat he was still wearing. "Christmas."

Addisyn tore her attention from her thousand-yard stare down with the table to look at Henry and then to me. She flipped her hair as if she was clearing the thoughts from her head. "Like Christmas beats Halloween?"

"I don't know," I said. "I don't know what's true or not anymore. Dad told me one story and some of the townsfolk told me another. Either way, the gist of it was Mom taunted the damn thing by covering the house with Christmas decorations. At least that's what I've been told."

Addisyn said, "Maybe it don't like it 'cause it's the opposite."

"'Cause everyone is cheery?" Henry asked her. "All happy when everyone is scared on Halloween."

"Nah," she said, "'Cause it's opposite. What's Halloween all about?" She didn't give him time to answer. "Takin'. The kiddies are takin' candy and bein' mean little bastards playin' tricks on people. But Christmas is 'bout given' and doin' good deeds for people in need. Maybe Christmas bothers it 'cause it's the reverse."

Henry laughed. "Y'all shoulda named it the Grinch."

Addisyn suddenly became hyper. She stabbed the two fingers holding her cigarette in the air toward Henry and ashes fell onto the kitchen table. "'Xactly like the Grinch! Don't want nobody to be happy."

I said, "I don't think a good deed is going to kill it."

Henry slammed back the last of his beer before crushing the can

one-handed. He belched and said, "Good deed never killed anyone."
He laughed.

"Would be worth a try," Addisyn said.

"No good deed goes unpunished," I added before pushing my
chair from the table. I wasn't sure if I was tired or slightly buzzed as
I stumbled and gripped the table. The pyramid of beer cans jum-
bled but somehow managed to not fall. "Sorry, folks, I think I'm
done for." The other two groaned in protest. "You're more than welcome to stay up but it's way past my bedtime. You know where everything is. Mi casa es su casa."

Henry's face screwed up into a confused and angry expression.
"What in the hell is that s'pose to mean?"

"Means we do whatever the fuck we want, stupid," Addisyn said.

The two bickered as I crossed the kitchen and descended the
basement stairs. My brain was foggy from the sleep deprivation and
alcohol but I thought, right before I fell into a dreamless slumber,
the bickering morphed into conspiratorial whispers.

FIFTEEN

TWO COMPETING REPETITIOUS SOUNDS PULLED me from a deep sleep. One was the loudest snore I'd ever encountered coming from somewhere upstairs. The other was the shrill ring of the kitchen wall phone. At first, I tried to ignore the ringing but the caller persisted. We'd never owned an answering machine, no need for it, but in that moment I wished we did.

I wasn't sure how long the phone rang before I convinced myself the caller wasn't going to hang up. I knew whatever reason they were calling must be important for them to be ringing shortly after sunrise. My neck tensed when I lifted my head from the pillow and a shot of white-hot pain streaked across the top of my skull and into my left eye. I wasn't sure if it was the pain or the hangover that made my stomach roll as I sat up.

The pain in my head and neck were worse once I was on my feet. The discordant opposing rhythms of the snoring and the ringing phone made me want to vomit as I climbed the basement stairs. The daylight, although scant, made the pain flair once I opened the door and stepped into the kitchen. I hurriedly lifted the phone from the receiver to alleviate one thing from the growing list of offending senses wreaking havoc on my battered brain. In my haste I fumbled with the receiver and nearly dropped it.

I squeezed my eyes shut and leaned my forehead against the

wall and said, "Hello?" My voice cracked and was thick with sleep.

"Barry!" the voice barked.

I pulled the phone a few inches from my ear and dry heaved. I took a deep breath, hoping I wouldn't vomit. "Yeah," I replied.

"Barry," Grayson said again, less of a shout. "Got a call from Janice. Said y'all had a visit last night."

My mind reeled as I tried to compose an excuse. I must have let the silence go on too long.

"Barry," he said firmly. "I sure hope that's not the case. It'd be a damn shame if your hospitality to those folks yer entertainin' included an introduction to our town secret. I mean . . . shit, boy, ya only had one job. I jus' don't know what I'm gonna do with the three of ya but I can't imagine it'd be anythin' y'all'd be comfortable with . . . and on the very day of the fall festival. Folks is lookin' forward to those rides—"

"Nothing happened," I blurted.

The aggravated sigh the sheriff let out distorted and popped through the earpiece, forcing me to pull the receiver from my ear again.

"Nothin' happened," he said. "Now why would Janice call me all in a panic if nothin' happened?"

Down the hall, the snoring was interrupted by a fit of wet coughs, sounding like Addisyn.

I didn't know what to say. Tell him I lied to save my ass? To save Henry and Addisyn? Tell him I got drunk and stupid and I'm a lonely and depressed old man who was looking for someone to share my Kafkaesque looping nightmare of a life with so I didn't feel like I was losing my last ounce of sanity after losing my father and being threatened by him and forced to work slave labor for the town and being the person who damned another human being to whatever fate Halloween had in store for them? He probably didn't know what the word Kafkaesque meant and would drive over here in a minute to kick my ass for 'tryin' to get smart with him'.

"Barry!"

Flabbergasted, I resorted to the excuse I'd heard a million times over the years for Janice's nosiness. "Janice is off her rocker."

"She is, is she?"

"Yeah. She stands in the window every night while Halloween is out. I'm pretty sure she enjoys watching it kill her cats. A little demented, if you ask me."

Now the awkward silence came from his end. I was compelled to add more but wasn't sure if he was buying it. If I kept rambling on with a list of Janice's offenses I knew I'd sound like I was deflecting, which I was. The silence made me nervous and I couldn't help myself from adding more.

I said, "She seemed a little too enthusiastic to talk to Henry and Addisyn as we approached my house yesterday. I hurried them inside though. I was afraid of what she might say to them. If you ask me, I think she has a bit of dementia setting in."

"Well," he said, "I sure hope you're right." He didn't sound completely convinced. "Be a damn shame if word got out 'bout Strang."

I thought, *Would it though? Be a shame?* Maybe if the world knew, something could be done about Halloween. Maybe we'd all be given refuge somewhere far away and when no one was left to play Halloween's games, what would become of it?

"Place would be swarmin'," he said. "All kinds of weirdoes and boogeyman catchers runnin' amok. A recipe for disaster. Someone bound to get hurt. A *lot* of people bound to get hurt. And we wouldn't want that, would we, Barry?"

"No, sir."

"Good." He took a deep breath and let it out slowly. "A'ight, I'll keep an eye on Janice. Wouldn't want nothin' to ruin the festival today."

I agreed with him before he disconnected. I stared at the phone for a second. "Goddammit, Janice," I whispered.

My head throbbed three beats with Addisyn's every snore. I retrieved some aspirin from the bathroom, leaving the bottle on the edge of the sink in case anyone else woke up in the same state as me, and drank a large glass of water before attempting to return to bed. As I was about to retreat to the dark and cool basement, a movement in the living room caught my attention.

A lone guinea pig sat in the middle of the living room floor, staring at me. It didn't bother to run as I approached it. I stooped to pick up the animal and the throbbing in my head intensified. When I stepped up to the cages, I couldn't find a single door open. My brain didn't want to try to figure out how the little guy had escaped.

Addisyn or Henry must have let it out and forgot to return it. I set him in the proper enclosure and collapsed on the sofa, staring at the guinea pigs, wondering how wonderful it must be to not have a care in the world. These were the last of my thoughts as I fell asleep on the sofa.

SIXTEEN

I WOKE TO THE SOUND of Henry shuffling out of his room. He was in his whitey tighties. He slid his feet on the floor as he headed for the bathroom, hair disheveled and bleary eyed. He scratched his scrotum and passed gas before entering the bathroom.

My headache had receded to manageable. I headed toward the kitchen to start breakfast. Addisyn roused after Henry left the bathroom.

By the time the two of them joined me in the kitchen the coffee was brewing, the scrambled eggs were almost done, and I was trying to avoid being popped by bacon grease. Bread sprung from the toaster and I set a jug of orange juice on the table between the two. Addisyn snatched the jug and chugged straight from it before handing it to Henry who did the same. It didn't look like I would be getting any.

The two looked worn but no more than anyone who'd just woken up. Neither looked as bad as I'd felt the first time I'd gotten up to answer the phone and I imagined they were pros at drinking the quantity we had last night. They looked to be the type who drank that much every night.

Once I'd set plates of food on the table they dug in, scarfing down the food as if they hadn't eaten in days. They didn't make eye contact or speak to me and I assumed they weren't morning people.

I felt bad for speaking up.

"The sheriff called this morning," I said.

Henry didn't deviate from eating. Addisyn stopped to look at me.

"I guess my neighbor saw us last night interacting with Halloween."

Henry stopped shoveling food into his mouth and looked at me, slowly chewing his bacon. I didn't elaborate and let what I'd said sink in.

"What's that mean?" Addisyn said.

I shrugged. "I told him the neighbor is a loony and making things up. I don't know exactly what would happen if he knew you two knew but he made it sound like it wasn't something good and I'd be joining you."

Henry and Addisyn looked at one another before slowly turning back to their plates.

Henry said, "Be kinda hard to explain our disappearance to the guys when they came to retrieve the rides."

Neither one of them offered any more commentary, which I found a bit odd but chalked it up to too much drinking and them being the type who wanted to be left alone before having their coffee.

We finished our breakfast in silence and each went about getting ready to spend the majority of the day at the festival. I spent too much time staring in the mirror in the bathroom after the shower, berating my conscience about the dot and my part in it. Once we were all showered and fed it was close to 10:30. I led them uptown since they'd told me they needed to do some pre-operating inspections of the rides before anyone was allowed on them.

The air was filled with the smell of sugar and grease and all the delicious aromas that filled the food area for any carnival or circus. It was a smell I'd associated with Halloween since my childhood. I spotted Rhonda pouring more sugar in the cotton candy machine as our trio made its way to the rides.

I hung back and watched Henry and Addisyn fire up the rides. The few townies setting up their part of the festival stopped what they were doing to watch in wonder as the light and sounds of the rides filled the town square. Purple and green and red and blue lights bounced dimly off the buildings and I knew they'd be a more spectacular sight once the sun set and gave way to full dark. A blast of heavy metal music a decade old came over the speakers mounted on either side of the Alien Abduction sign and Addisyn began to nod her head rigorously as Henry mimed playing a guitar near the entrance of the Tilt-A-Whirl.

I couldn't help but observe Rhonda as her face filled with the excitement of a small child. There was something about her expression that made her look years younger than she was. Even though her smile made the wrinkles around her eyes and mouth more prominent, you could see the innocent and carefree girl she was several decades past. Seeing her face lit up was something I hadn't seen in Strang for a long time . . . if ever. The faint colorful lights from the rides danced across her face as she watched them. She broke from the trance once the carnies shut them down and her face powered down quicker than the rides themselves. She turned back to preparing the food for the festival as if the small thrill she'd experienced had never happened.

Old Hurley called for me. He waved a clipboard in the air and pointed at it.

I let Addisyn and Henry know the volume of the music might be a bit much for the old folks, to which they waved at me dismissively. I told them Doris would probably ask for them to cut the music later once they needed to use the PA system to announce the costume contest and lottery winner.

Hurly became impatient with me to join him and called, "Baaaaaarrrrry!" I reluctantly approached him, knowing exactly what he wanted. "Ya wanna sign up for the tournament?" He held up the clipboard to show me the only name on it at the moment was his own.

I'd never played horseshoes in all my years. I wasn't one for competition and my ego was a fragile thing. And in my current state I was pretty certain having Hurley berate me in front of a handful of the other old farts in town might actually break me.

"No, thanks," I said. "I better find out what else Doris wants me to do before I commit to anything." I spotted Kathy sitting on a bench outside the grocery store, scowling at the lot of us with her arms folded tightly over her chest. I used her as an excuse to get away from him. "Be back. Going to see what Kathy is up to."

I crisscrossed through the festival displays, passing Bill and a few other people setting up the dreaded stage and testing the PA system. Kathy scrutinized me with a hateful squint as I stepped up onto the curb and neared her. I took a seat next to her on the bench.

"Whaddya want?" she said.

"Nothing. I can't take a break on the bench beside you? You're taking a break, right?"

"Guess so. Got another half hour before the store closes for the day. But you got that look like yer gonna ask me somethin'."

"What look?"

"Don't know. Jus' a look."

I shrugged and watched Bill struggle with the microphone stand before tapping the mic. No sound came from the speakers. A minute passed without Kathy or I speaking to one another.

"Dressing up?" I asked.

"Are you dressin' up?" she said. "Costumes are fer kiddies. I'm too old for that gobbledygook. They's jus' blowin' smoke up our asses anyhow."

I looked up at the overcast sky before asking, "Do you think there's any way to stop it?"

She let loose a half laugh, half bark. "They'd done tooken care of it if there was."

"What about Christmas?"

"What 'bout it?"

I thought about Addisyn and Henry's theory of Halloween and Christmas being opposites and how one could possibly cancel the other. The battle of good versus evil. "Maybe we could fight Halloween with Christmas."

She let out a hardy laugh. It drew the attention of the people assisting Bill. Once she settled down she sighed and shook her head. "That's the most asinine thing I've ever heard."

"But you said so yourself my mom was trying to stop it. And she put out all those decorations and it made Halloween real mad. Maybe she was on to something."

"Oh, dear lord," she said. She lifted her face to the sky as if she actually were addressing a god. She looked at me. "It's mad 'bout everything. It thrives off makin' people miserable. Playin' tricks and all."

"Maybe we should all ignore it then. If we don't give it an audience it can't torture us."

"Where is all this comin' from?"

"I don't know."

She really scrutinized me then. "No. There's somethin' goin' on with you. You look . . . I don't know. Real bad. Like you ain't slept or somethin'."

I tried to gauge the distance between us and Bill and his crew. I was certain they wouldn't be able to hear us but I also noticed Grayson had stepped out of the police station and was staring me down.

The sheriff reluctantly tore his eyes from me and slowly meandered down the street toward Rhonda.

I said under my breath, "If I tell you something you promise not to tell anyone else?"

She said, "Why you whisperin'?" louder than her normal volume.

I patted my hands slightly in a sign for her to keep it down. "Don't announce it to the whole town."

"What?"

Barely moving my lips, afraid someone might be able to read them, I said, "I was in charge of labeling the envelopes."

She gasped and leaned away from me abruptly, as if I was about to hit her.

I made a disgruntled sound. "Would you keep it down?"

"Keep it down? I ain't actin' a fool."

I wanted to say 'could've fooled me' but thought better of it. "I'm not supposed to let anyone know. It has been eating me up. Knowing I'm going to be responsible for someone's life tonight. I don't know how I'm going to be able to live with myself after Halloween has come and taken . . ." I didn't want to say the words 'kill' or 'eaten alive' or any of the other horrifying things the people of Strang thought happened to the person whose name was on the envelope containing the dot. I stared at Bill and wondered if he already knew who it was. Surely Doris let the town committee know. "Just seems like there has to be a way to stop it."

"Like I said. They would've done it by now if they knew. We's jus' gonna have to eventually die out. That's it. When we're all dead, it'll die."

"I don't know. What's to say it won't move on to the next town?"

She shrugged. "There ain't no tellin'."

SEVENTEEN

THE TOWNSFOLK BEGAN TO TRICKLE in a few minutes before noon. In almost the blink of an eye the square was filled with people milling about. A group of men swarmed the horseshoe area and most of the women convened around the food tables. Small lines formed for the rides, which I found surprising, but most of the elderly were in line for the hayride. The whole area was overrun by chatter and the music blasting from the Alien Abduction ride. A few of the elderly squinted hatefully at the speakers blaring the music, as if they could will the music to cut out or change it to something more suitable to their tastes.

Several of the middle-aged women were dressed for the contest and a few people had even made costumes. I spotted a couple ghosts fashioned from old bedsheets. One moved fairly slowly with the assistance of a cane. Rhonda had changed at some point before people began to arrive and was now dressed as a popular slasher movie monster, including a worn brown hat and modified glove, the latter appearing to hinder her ability to deal with the food.

Out of nowhere a small figure clad all in black materialized at my side, waving their arms in my face and yowling. My attention had been focused on Rhonda and the person startled me as they accosted me. My chest was tight and painful from the fright and I took a step back before I realized the personal space invader was

Janice.

"What are you doing?" I said. I rubbed my chest, thinking the action would lessen the pain. "You scared me half to death."

A few people nearby took notice of the commotion she was invoking but were just as quickly disinterested and moved on.

"Yowl. Meow," she said.

She ran her hands up and down in front of my face. Her already gnarled and arthritic fingers were curled into claws. It took a second for me to fully absorb her costume. She wore a full spandex leotard that was doing nothing for her elderly figure, nor leaving a square inch to the imagination. Her mask was shiny black with white stitching and pointed ears. The whole ensemble made me really uncomfortable. I was certain she wasn't wearing a bra and the garment was pulled taut enough to be see-through. She was clearly wearing an incontinence undergarment, which was bunched and puffy under the costume.

"I'm a catty woman," Janice said. "Meow. Meow."

"Yeah," I said testily and looked everywhere but at her. "I get it."

She stopped pawing at me. "I saw Halloween stop by your place last night."

An old man slowly making his way to take a seat on a haystack near us stopped and looked at us a moment before turning and heading in a different direction. I didn't know what to do but I sure as hell didn't want her telling people about what she saw. Sheriff Grayson was dubious of my story and I didn't want her to give him a reason to interrogate either one of us. Janice was a little off anyway and I chose to gaslight her.

"I don't know what you're talking about," I said.

"Last night. Old Halloween came a knockin'." She gave me a huge smile, which caused her dentures to slip, and she was forced to suck them back and close her mouth to reattach them to her gums.

"Last night I was entertaining the carnies. There was no Halloween."

"Entertainin' them by showin' them the boogeyman," she taunted.

I turned and stared her hard in the eye. "No. I. Didn't. I don't know what you think you saw but maybe you need your eyes checked, Janice." I hissed her name to emphasize my frustration with her.

"Oh, ha ha. You're a testy one. Jus' like your mama. That's why I called the sheriff. You'll bring Halloween down on the whole town you keep actin' a fool."

I wanted to yell in her face how I wished the earth would open up and swallow the whole damn town if it meant I wasn't responsible for someone's fate tonight and it meant I never had to talk to her or Grayson ever again and I never had to pick up some dumb, poor creature and place it on my stoop for that monster one more night. If it meant I didn't have to be reminded of Mom or go home to an empty house and be reminded of my part in Dad's death. I wanted it all to fall into oblivion and the whole thing to be put out of its misery.

"Doesn't matter," I said. "He thinks you're the crazy old coot you really are." I turned and stormed off toward Henry's ride, not wanting to give her a chance to respond.

"Wouldn't be so sure 'bout that," Janice called after me.

I wasn't thinking of much more than trying to get away from Janice. There was nothing appealing about getting on any of the rides to me but at least it'd give me a chance to be alone. There wasn't much more to do that didn't involve some sort of interaction with another person. But if I was seated by myself in a ride car I could at least get some peace and quiet for a few minutes.

I was in line for the Tilt-A-Whirl before I knew it, staring hard at the red and drab green stripes of the sweater on the person in front of me. I checked the town clock and noted there was less than a half hour before the sun slipped over the horizon. I turned to stare at the back of the person in front of me again. When they turned their head I noticed a bright red lock of hair fall down their back. I was standing behind Rhonda. I turned to the food cart and spotted Kathy behind the counter, handing someone a funnel cake.

Rhonda waved weakly to someone in the crowd before turning and spotting me. She looked a bit startled. "Hi," she said.

My face grew hot. But not as much as it normally did when I spoke to her. My mind was too buried in all the other worries on my mind to be fully embarrassed. "Hello."

"Havin' fun?"

I shrugged and stared at the ground.

Out of the corner of my eye I noticed she shrugged in response and turned up one corner of her mouth to give me a lopsided smile. She said, "'Bout as much fun as one can have with the closing ceremonies an' all, huh?"

"I guess," I managed. She had me tongue-tied. Having a conversation with her was the last thing I expected and not a top priority. She probably assumed my clipped responses were either the result of me being an idiot or a socially awkward jackass. The latter of which I wouldn't argue with.

We were interrupted by Henry hollering the rules at us as the previous riders exited their carts and made their way out into the crowd of attendees. I don't know why I'd thought getting on the ride was the best place to find a bit of solitude. I didn't have a particular urge to be flung around to the beat of heavy metal music while sulking in my own plight. This was all Janice's fault. If she hadn't gotten me all flabbergasted at being exposed to Grayson and causing me to run off . . .

I was about to step out of the line but Henry beckoned the crowd forward and began dividing the people up into groups of two or three and assigning them to a cart. The folks behind me closed in and I was pushed forward. I bumped into Rhonda and apologized.

When Rhonda reached Henry he asked, "How many?"

"Oh, uh." She turned around and looked at me and the person behind me.

I turned to find another couple standing behind me.

"Two," she said.

I asked, "Can I get my own. I don't want to smash anyone." It was true. I was overweight and the thought of pinning Rhonda against some painted-over, rusted metal with my girth mortified me. That and it would rescue me from having to socialize or pretend to be happy around anyone, especially Rhonda.

The corner of Henry's mouth twitched almost imperceptibly. I was an idiot if I didn't think he was going to let me get out of being alone with Rhonda. He knew how I felt about her but what he didn't realize was he wasn't doing me any favors. He said, "Ain't that kinda ride, Barry."

"It's fine," Rhonda said. "It's okay if—"

Someone behind us complained loudly about what was taking so long.

"Okay," I said, resigned. "Just . . . do what you have to." My request was causing the situation to get more awkward by the moment.

Henry pointed at a car on the other side. Rhonda and I made our way around the ride and seated ourselves. Neither of us spoke as Henry made his way to each car and locked everyone in. As the ride fired up I spotted Grayson standing off to the side of the line, his hands on the waist-high metal gate separating the contraption from the crowd, staring me down. I wanted to shout, 'Goddamn it! Can't I go anywhere and be left in peace?!' but I knew it wouldn't accomplish anything but ruining everyone's good time and singling me out as the crazy guy who lost his shit at the fall festival the one year.

The ride began to gain speed and our cart rotated lackadaisically as we neared Grayson. Once we were past him he turned to scrutinize Henry.

I thought, *Damn it! Damn it! Damn it! He's going to give Henry the third degree.*

I'd only known Henry a day and a half so I didn't know how he would deal with the sheriff or how the sheriff would deal with him. I surely didn't want Henry and Addisyn to suffer for any of my poor decisions. And as awful as I felt for thinking it, I didn't think Henry was the sharpest tool in the shed. The sheriff was bound to trip him up one way or another.

Rhonda whooped and laughed as the ride went on. I tried to follow her direction and make the cart swing the way she wanted but I was entirely too nervous to enjoy it or the satisfaction she was getting. I was too worried about keeping an eye on the sheriff. Grayson eventually wandered off without speaking a word to Henry, which made me feel slightly better. But I knew deep in my gut the sheriff was determined to nail my ass high and dry and make an example out of me one way or another.

Once the ride stopped I didn't wait for Henry. The bar dug into my gut as I leaned toward the pin near my foot. I unpinned the safety and lifted the bar to free the two of us. I didn't pay any mind to Rhonda as I hastily exited the car. I stepped down from the ride and carefully hopped over the fence separating the flailing hunk of metal from the rest of the crowd. Someone expressed their dismay as I bumped into them. I didn't bother excusing myself as I weaved through the crowd, bumping into people and stepping on a few toes, as I headed toward home.

I knew it was against the rules to stay home during the festival but I couldn't take it. My head was a mess and it seemed like, no matter what I did, Grayson had it out for me anyway. If he was bound and determined to make my life a living hell I might as well make it worth it. I was halfway to the house when I noticed it. Something in the air changed drastically.

I stopped so quickly I almost tripped and fell. A painful chill rain down my spine and a sharp pain shot through my chest. I didn't have to look at my watch to know the sun had fallen beyond the horizon. The sky was already the shade of dark you knew like the back of your hand if you lived in Strang. Everyone here had an impeccable internal clock. The question was: how long had the sun been down?

"Barry," a terrible voice hissed behind me. "Where are you going?" Its tone was mocking. And I knew in that moment the sun had been down long enough for Halloween to find me. "Don't you want to join in the fun? Oh, what fun it is." It laughed low and the sound was almost a growl before it began to recite, "Monsters, stalking through the night, Halloween is the night of fright. Fear is what this night brings, along with many other things. Are you sure you are prepared? Tonight is not for the easily scared. Creatures from hell roam on this night, for tonight is the Night of Fright."

"Shut up," I said. My delivery was more pathetic than I anticipated. I didn't want to turn toward it. I didn't want to see it. I didn't want to confront it. I wanted it to go away.

Its voice grew in volume. "Trick-or-treat you say, you should not have waited until the end of the day. Tonight you will lose your tricks and treats, for the monsters need to eat."

My heart began to hammer. I placed my hands over my ears and began to cower. I didn't want to hear the damn thing and I was certain I was seconds away from losing my life regardless of any agreement the people of Strang had with Halloween and tonight's events. The thing had it out for me.

I felt the unnaturalness of it as it placed its mouth next to my ear, almost a vibration, which complemented the constant blur it appeared to be to most people. It delivered the last of the rhyme mere inches from my ear, which rang crystal clear even with my hands covering them. It said, "You better not take this night lightly, or else you will truly learn what fright means. In ancient times people feared this night, the night they greeted with fright. Why they were so scared you will soon see, on this All Hallows' Eve."

I screamed, trying to block out its voice.

It laughed. "You'd be well advised to return to the festivities. I wouldn't want you to miss out on all the fun."

The most intense pain I'd ever experienced ripped through my chest and down my arm. I let go of my ears to clutch my chest with one arm. I went down on my knees and put my free hand on the ground to catch myself from faceplanting on the sidewalk. Each breath I took ignited another bolt of pain. I tried to take smaller breaths but the pain was so excruciating it caused me to gasp and tamped out my efforts for the tiniest bit of relief.

The thing took the opportunity to whoop and dance around me as I collapsed to the sidewalk. It was so difficult to breathe and I managed to roll onto my back even though I didn't want to see Halloween taking any enjoyment in my predicament. The sidewalk was ice cold and bit at my skin as I gasped like a fish out of water. Nausea washed over me as the pain intensified even more, which I didn't think was possible.

I'm having a heart attack.

The creature bent over me and revealed what I believed to be its true face. The flashes of light, the blackened heart, all teeth and claws. The hideous thing grinned at me, knowing I was dying. It gave a childish giggle as red and black dots swam around the edges of my vision and everything began to darken. I could've sworn from the pain I was experiencing Halloween was sitting on my chest but it only crouched over me.

This is it.

I'm dying.

And the last thing I'll ever see is this sadistic creature taking pleasure in my demise.

Why me?

I wish I would've asked Rhonda out.
I hope when it eats me it gets sick and dies.
I hope I taste bitter.
I should've moved away a long time ago.
I hate Strang.
I miss my mom.

Something I could only describe as a miniscule pop happened in my chest before the pain ceased and the world went black.

EIGHTEEN

SOMETHING HARD HIT MY RIBS. "Get up."

I opened my eyes to darkness. Not complete darkness. The streetlamps were lit but the sky beyond was full dark. I hadn't realized the moon was supposed to be full tonight and so blindingly bright. The moon was as luminous as the sun and moving. I lifted my arm weakly to shield my eyes from it.

"I said get up," Grayson said firmly.

It took a few more seconds for me to get my bearings back and remember what happened. The light wasn't the moon or the sun. It was Grayson's flashlight. I was still alive. And the real moon hung low in the sky and was actually full or nearly full. I never paid much attention to the cycle of the moon and couldn't be completely sure.

Grayson deliberately delivered a stiff kick to my ribs as motivation for me to move.

"Boy, I feared you'd go yella on me but I kept tellin' myself 'that boy ain't got the cojones'. Now you get yer ass off the ground and get back to the square before I shoot ya."

I tried to roll onto my side but I was weak and shaky. I mumbled, "I think I had a heart attack."

"Wish you would have a heart attack," Grayson said. "Save me and the town a huge headache. Ya been nothin' but a boil on my ass since yer daddy died. Struttin' around makin' a ruckus." He bent to get closer to me as I flayed weakly on the ground, trying to get the strength to stand. "Janice might be as crazy as a shit house rat but I don't think she hallucinated what she saw last night." He shook his finger in my face. "And if I find out you's breakin' the town rules I'm liable to drag your ass behind a barn and give ya two to the back of the head. Strang's got enough worries without me havin' to keep an eye on some asshole who wants to play the goddamn hero 'round here." He stood erect and delivered another kick to my ribs. "Now you get your lard ass up and get back to the square. It's almost time for the dot and I know how much you'll wanna be there for that."

I'd made it to a sitting position, and as I tried to stand, Grayson became impatient with me. He grabbed my upper arm and jerked me up to my feet. I wouldn't have thought a scrawny old man like himself would've been able to lift someone my size. I took a few tentative steps back toward the square. My bones and muscles felt as though they'd been removed, pulverized in a blender, and poured back into my skin. I was afraid I'd collapse if I moved too quickly. My chest felt as though I'd taken a hard knock with a sledgehammer. It was a struggle to stay upright when Grayson became impatient with the speed of my progress and decided to give my back a hard shove as an incentive to walk faster.

As we neared the town square I realized the music from Addisyn's ride was no longer blaring. A voice was talking over the loudspeaker but I couldn't quite make out what they were saying. A loud cheer erupted and startled me. Once we rounded the corner I found the townspeople had abandoned the festival activities and were crowded around the makeshift stage.

Henry and Addisyn stood at the control panel for the Tilt-A-Whirl, whispering to one another and smoking. Addisyn spotted Grayson and me first and said something to Henry before giving her head a flick and taking a hit of her smoke. They looked worried and hardened, as if they were ready for battle, and I wasn't sure if it was for me or something else. I started toward them but Grayson grabbed my arm and marched me to the back of the crowd.

He let go of my arm and stayed beside me. He whispered, "Yer gonna wanna be close to the stage." He gave me a smarmy smile before folding his arms across his chest and redirecting his attention to the stage.

Bill was on the stage, holding a microphone lowered from his mouth. Janice was on stage with him, pawing at the air in the same manner she'd done to me earlier. She danced about as gracefully as an elderly woman could and I was pretty sure she was meowing like a cat. A gold ribbon was pinned above one saggy breast on her tight suit.

Bill lifted the microphone to his mouth and belted out, "Let's give it up for Ms. Janice! This year's first-place costume winner!" The volume of his voice distorted what he said.

The crowd erupted into cheers and whistles as Janice made her way down the wooden steps and joined the crowd. Doris took the stage and the excitement of the crowd settled down quickly. Aside from a few coughs you might've been able to hear a pin drop. There was a considerable shift in the mood of the crowd and a low dreadful sensation of something unholy. Some of the crowd looked around worriedly, knowing the sensation was Halloween, hiding in the shadows or around the corner of a building, waiting for his ultimate treat to be handed over, never revealing itself to the festival attendees.

I turned around and spotted Henry and Addisyn scanning the area. They had to have felt the sudden change in the air too. I spotted a blur of movement beyond the carnies, rounding the rides and crouching low to the ground, before it slipped down a narrow alley between two buildings. Grayson elbowed me in the ribs, hard. I stifled a yelp and rubbed the offended spot. A couple people in front of me looked at me, confused and annoyed, before redirecting their attention to the stage.

On stage, Doris took the microphone from Bill. She said, "Hello! Welcome, everyone, to the annual fall festival!"

A round of halfhearted applause trickled through the crowd.

"I'd like to thank everyone for attending this year," she said. "And thank you to everyone who volunteered their time to help set up and run the whole affair. I want to give a special thanks to Wacky Times Amusements." She held her hand out in the direction of the amusement rides. "Please, let's give it up to Henry and Addisyn for being such good sports with our limited situation."

The crowd gave a pathetic and unenthusiastic round of applause.

Doris continued, "I hope everyone enjoyed the rides. We hope to bring you all more things like this in the future."

A smaller round of applause rippled through the crowd. Someone in front of me grunted 'hurry up'.

"Remember," she added, "if you'd like to give any suggestions or recommendations for next year's fall festival be sure to attend our town meetings."

Somewhere in the middle of the crowd Old Hurley shouted, "I got a suggestion! Get on with it!"

A few people chuckled.

Doris' speech became clipped. "It appears everyone is ready for the next part. I guess we should move on to the dot then." She fished around in the pocket of her jacket and retrieved a piece of paper.

The few people fidgeting in the horde stopped. Everyone seemed to collectively hold their breath as Doris shook the paper to unfold it. She held the paper at arm's length to read it since she didn't have her reading glasses on. She squinted at the writing as if she didn't already know whose name was printed on it. She and Grayson were the ones who opened the envelopes. I couldn't be sure why she was putting on such a theatrical display of revealing the name. To give the unlucky person three more seconds to live? To put the whole town through three more seconds of agony as each person dreaded hearing their name called?

"As decreed by the village of Stang," she said. "I hereby do announce the winner of this year's dot drawing to be . . ." She dropped the microphone from her mouth and looked out over the townspeople as if she were looking for the person she was about to call.

I spotted a woman clasping a hand over her mouth as if it would contain whatever horrors might fall from her lips if her name was chosen. A shock of red hair partially hidden under a brown hat in the middle of the group caught my attention. Rhonda stood stock-still among the people. A surge of panic crept into my already weakened chest at the thought of her name being called. Doris appeared to give up on her search and lifted the microphone to her mouth.

"This year's winner of the dot is Barry Johnson!"

My heart stopped. My face went numb. My body went numb. If whatever happened earlier—let's call it a heart attack for argument's sake—hadn't killed me, I was hoping the shock of hearing my name called would cause some internal phenomena to kill me where I stood. Behind me, I barely registered shocked sounds from Henry and Addisyn. A few people in the crowd clapped and some others cried out in relief.

A hand clamped down hard on my shoulder and almost knocked me to the ground in my shocked state of weakness.

Grayson whispered in my ear, "Congratulations, shithead." He turned his head to look behind us and I knew he was observing the carnies before he turned back to me.

I turned to him and blinked rapidly, trying to process what was about to happen, trying to process what *had* happened. Grayson smiled at me with an expression of pure contempt and delight.

My mouth had gone dry but I managed to whisper back, "You did this."

His smile became lopsided and morphed into a knowing and se-cretive smile. It wasn't a lottery. They chose who they felt like get-ting rid of. I didn't know if this was the case every year. But they surely made an exception this year or at least Grayson was making it a point for it to appear that way to me.

"You . . . bastard," I managed. "Why do you hate me so much?"

The sheriff turned and shouted toward the stage. "Here he is! Winner, winner, chicken dinner!"

The entire group turned to look at me. Everyone was eerily qui-et and, without being prompted, opened a path through the center of the crowd for me to approach the stage. The sheriff squeezed my upper arm and dug his fingers in so hard it felt as if four knives were working their way to the bone.

"Come on," he said. "Get goin'."

The shock of what was happening made my body vibrate. My legs were like jelly. Everything sped up and slowed down at the same time. I barely registered the faces as I was ushered toward the stage. I got a glimpse of Kathy and Mr. McCallister standing beside one another. Their faces were ashen and the first signs of worry and grief were beginning to set into their features. I couldn't look at them and redirected my gaze toward the stage where Doris stood waiting. She appeared blurry before I realized tears were threatening to spill from my eyes. I was trying to come to terms with my impending death. If I could make myself accept the fact it would all be over soon and not think about any pain that might be involved with my eradication, maybe it wouldn't be so bad. I was grasping for some sort of zen to keep me from losing it. I began to hyperventilate and then spotted the shock of red hair. Rhonda was standing among the people along my path to Halloween. She'd clasped a hand over her mouth and tears rimmed her eyes.

Grayson still had hold of my upper arm and was marching me along. When I came to a full stop he kicked out a leg as if to steady himself from falling and spun toward me. I jerked my arm from his grip. And he looked equal parts angry and excited.

"Boy—" he warned me.

I cut him off. "This isn't right. You know it isn't."

"Now, don't you go givin' me no grief." He played up his speech for those close to us. "Rules is rules. Ain't nobody ever given us no trouble. You know the deal." He looked around at the people surrounding us. "We *all* know the deal. If ya didn't want to play by the rules you shoulda moved outta town—"

"You!" I shouted and pointed at him. I took a breath to calm myself. "You wouldn't let me."

His patience had grown thin. He pulled his gun from its holster. "Now I've had 'bout 'nough of yer smart aleck mouth."

People nearest to us began to back away and a few gasps came from the crowd.

"What? You're going to shoot me? What about the carnies? Seems sorta dumb to go through all this trouble to keep everything a secret from them only to give me the dot or gun me down like a dog. Are you gonna shoot them too?"

He cocked the gun. "Don't make no difference. When they're friends show up tomorrow they might find their friends up and left in the middle of the night. Or maybe they had an accident dealin' with those contraptions. Ain't no sense in keepin' up the ruse when ya done told them everything."

I was about to protest their innocence when he looked beyond me toward the rides.

He said, "Looks like they already abandoned ya anyhow." He

lifted the gun and pointed it at my face.

The gasps from the people echoed off the buildings. A woman screamed somewhere toward the front of the crowd. The group gave us a wider berth. I couldn't help but notice Rhonda standing rooted to her spot, hand still clasped over mouth, now alone in the middle of the open aisle.

"Now, if ya'd rather expire here on the street I'd gladly help ya with that."

"You kill me," I said, "and you'll have to pick someone else for Halloween."

He shrugged. "Don't matter." He turned to look at the stage where Doris stood wringing her hands. His attention went to Rhonda before he turned back to me. "Now, are you gonna go quietly or am I gonna shoot you and give Halloween that—" he inclined his head in Rhonda's direction "—waitress ya always pinin' over."

I opened my mouth to say something when I spotted the blur beyond him, beyond Rhonda, standing beside the stage. A few of the other townsfolk near the stage must have sensed its presence and turned to spot Halloween too. The crowd shifted to get away from it. The townspeople were in a dilemma. No one wanted to be near Halloween but they were still concerned with the sheriff waving a gun around. They smashed each other against the buildings lining the street, stepping on one another, knocking a few elderly people who couldn't move fast enough to the ground.

The blur started creeping up behind Rhonda and the townsfolk shifted in kind to its position as it moved down the street.

"No!" I shouted.

The sheriff kept his gun trained on me but looked over his shoulder to see what caused me to yell. In one move, I grabbed Grayson's gun, wrenched his arm in one direction, and sidestepped in the opposite direction of the weapon. The blast was deafening and the gun kicked violently in his hand. The crowd went into full-blown panic mode. People began fleeing down the street.

I'd misjudged everything. I wasn't in the best physical shape to begin with but I was still weak from my collapse earlier. Grayson was wiry and *a lot* stronger than he appeared. He yanked his gun-holding hand from my grasp and slammed the butt of the weapon into my temple. I saw stars and then the pavement. I thought I'd smashed my forehead on the concrete but I couldn't be sure because the pain from Grayson's blow was immense. I'd managed to lift myself to my knees and elbows before Grayson delivered a kick to my ribs that knocked the air out of me. I fell on my side. I weakly rolled onto my back, trying to regain my breath.

There was a great deal of commotion from the crowd. Gasps, cries, and shrieks were creating a cacophony of terror throughout the square. People were scattering and cowering on the sidewalks. I spotted Rhonda in the same spot and the blur was shifting into something more solid as it approached us. Grayson cursed me and was about to deliver another kick to my ribs when Halloween quickly materialized beside him. The thing appeared in what I was certain was its true form. Its chest strobed and throbbed in flashes of orange light. It was almost twice as tall as Grayson. The sheriff stopped with his leg poised to deliver another strike and slowly looked up at it. The thing sneered down at him. It opened its mouth and hissed at him as a glob of drool dropped from its lip. The sheriff went white as a sheet.

This wasn't how this normally went. Halloween never revealed itself during the festival. And, other than the few times at my house, it had never shown itself in this form. Every other year the name was called and the person was escorted off so the other townsfolk could finish out the night's festivities or hang around drinking until they passed out in the street or just stay up and outside until the sun came up, since it was the one night of the year they were allowed to do so. But there was nothing normal about this year's transaction.

The thing squatted. As Halloween lowered itself it kept its eyes on the sheriff. Once it was on its haunches it scooped me off the ground, stood quickly, and slung me over its shoulder like a sack of potatoes. I tried to fight Halloween off but I was too disoriented from getting struck in the head and the vertigo was making me nauseated. Without a word to anyone, Halloween headed back in the direction he'd come from. We passed Rhonda and when we did something must have broke her from her spell and she took off running in the opposite direction. Rhonda fleeing and a dumbstruck Grayson standing in the middle of the square were the last things I observed before Halloween rounded the corning of a building.

We were engulfed by the shadowy residential streets before the creature began to sprint to the edge of town. The jostling made my head hurt worse and the speed at which we were traveling was making me more nauseated. I began to kick at the thing but it clasped one of its enormous hands around both of my ankles and squeezed hard. Something popped in my ankle and I screamed. The thing laughed and my chest grew tight. It was all too much. The darkness of the countryside swallowed us and it was comforting as my mind slipped into the darkness also.

NINETEEN

I WOKE TO A SOFT CLACKING and someone muttering delightedly. I lay on my back against something hard and cold. The deep and musty smell of earth filled my olfactory senses along with the foulest stench of rot I'd ever encountered. An orange light flickered across the misshapen and craggy ceiling. It took me a few seconds to recall what happened as my head swam and throbbed with pain. The strobing orange light nauseated me.

I lay as still as possible and closed my eyes, hoping the nausea would pass. I hoped Halloween hadn't noticed I was awake. I figured it would've done whatever it did to people as soon as we'd made it to this place. Maybe it was waiting for me to wake up so the thing could revel in its yearly ritual or torture me. I opened my eye to the tiniest slit and tried to take in my surroundings by turning my head slowly to the side.

It appeared we were in a large circular cave with one pitch black tunnel leading into it. Halloween stood beside a small campfire in the center. There was a large pile of rotten animals next to the fire and the thing was attempting to seat sloppily pieced together human skeletons around the fire on chairs made from bones. One chair was massive, like a throne, and it sat empty. I assumed it was Halloween's chair.

The skeletons weren't fake and they weren't the cleaned and

bound skeletons found in a doctor's office. They were crude, dirty, and irregular creations bound by limited resources: rope, yarn, strips of plastic sacks, old gum, wire, etc. Their ribs jutted in odd angles and most appeared to have lost their necks as their heads either lolled to one side or sat on their shoulders. One skeleton had two heads and another had three sets of arms like a demented Indian deity. Some of them wore articles of old and rotten clothing. There appeared to be a dozen or so of the creations. And in the faint light of the campfire, beyond the gathering of skeletons, the walls and ceiling were covered in bones, much like the Paris catacombs. In one corner there was a pile of unused bones.

It took me a moment to register the myriad tiny animal skeletons around the feet of the human skeletons. Halloween mumbled as it worked to arrange its grotesque creations. There was an awful sound coming from the campfire's direction. Not so much a sound but the sensation of sound. A vibration of the screams of sorrow and fear of the endless years of Halloween's reign accumulated in the cave. It chilled me to the bone and made me convulsively shiver, my teeth chattering.

Halloween heard me and turned to look at me. I clenched my jaw and squeezed my eyes shut, trying to will all that was happening, or about to happen, away. There wasn't even a beat before it was at close proximity to me.

"You're awake," it said. "Just in time for my party."

My breath hitched and I bit back the fear. I couldn't bring myself to open my eyes and look at it. Large clammy fingers wrapped around either side of my head and Halloween picked me up off the ground by my skull. The weight of my own body stretched my spine and I felt and heard several pops as the strain caused the joints to crack. I cried out in pain and grasped its wrists to alleviate the pressure. It laughed at me. My body swayed as it moved and, as much as I didn't want to look in the damn thing's eyes, I wanted to know where it was carrying me. Panic made my heart race and my chest hurt again and I feared I was about to be tossed into the fire.

The thing sneered at me as it carried me to the throne and dropped me roughly onto it. My tailbone hit the chair constructed of Halloween's previous victims and white-hot pain flashed up my spine. I yelp and leaned to one side. As my feet tried to find purchase, another flash of pain came from my ankle. I vaguely recalled the pop Halloween induced by squeezing my ankle but it was the least of my worries at the moment.

It stooped toward me. "You don't have a costume." It stepped over to the pile of rotting animals and chose a rabbit from the stack. Halloween inserted one long talon into the front of the rabbit's neck and slit open the animal before skinning it. It tossed the rabbit's carcass over its shoulder and it landed back in the pile, causing a few other dead and decaying animals to tumble down the side of the stack. Halloween approached me with the foul and bloody fur of the rabbit and gingerly turned the skin right-side out so the fur was on the outside. It held open the hole as it put the vacant fur on my head as if it were a hat.

I tried to wiggle away from the disgusting fur but Halloween growled, "Sit still or I'll skin you next."

I stopped but tears immediately sprung to my eyes. "You're a fucking ghoul!" I managed between sobs.

It laughed at me as it slid the cold and slimy rabbit fur on my head. "Now you're a bunny." It took a couple of steps back to observe me. It laughed again before clapping. Halloween turned to its dead companions and said, "Isn't it funny?" He got no response before he bellowed, "Isn't he funny? Here comes Peter Cottontail, hoppin' down the bunny trail, hippity hoppin', Easter's on its way." It laughed again.

One of the skeletons twitched and I thought it was a trick of the firelight as it danced across surfaces in the cave. The two-headed skeleton sat up straighter with a jerk and one of its mouths opened. The jaw bounced up and down in a rhythm as if replicating human laughter. Another skeleton keeled forward, gripping its stomach, and began slapping its knee. The *clack, clack, clack* of its amusement echoed through the cave. Within a few seconds all of Halloween's demented friends were animated into a raucous round of laughter. The sound of laughter itself was absent, aside from Halloween, and instead was replaced with the sound of creaking and snapping bones. Halloween cheered them on and clapped and in an instant they all stopped, as if their marionette strings were suddenly cut. They fell back against their chairs with such force that some of them lost limbs. The two-headed one lost one of its heads and the skull was so old and brittle it cracked in two when it hit the hard earth.

Halloween turned to me and its lips parted wide into a grin, revealing its terrible teeth. "Wasn't that fun?"

"Why? Why are you doing this?"

It began to recite some of the rhyme from before. "Are you sure you are prepared? Tonight is not for the easily scared. Creatures from hell roam on this night, for tonight is the Night of Fright. Trick or treat, you say, you should not have waited until the end of the day. Tonight you will lose your tricks and treats, for the monsters need to eat."

"Please don't," I said as tears streamed down my face. "There has to be another way. You can have all my guinea pigs—"

"I don't want your tiny animals. Tonight I feed on the essence of something bigger. The fear of a human. Something conscious of death. That understands the concept of it. An animal knows nothing more than danger. It cannot understand it's about to die. It only understands pain and the avoidance of pain. But you—" It grabbed me on either side of my head and lifted me off the chair before it put its face close to mine. "Your fear will keep me here for another year."

I gripped its wrists again to take the weight off my neck. It felt as if my head would rip from my body. Halloween's eyes were even more horrid up close. They were like shining, soulless marbles as the light from its chest and the campfire light danced on their glossy surface. In my periphery I spotted the skeletons come to attention and stand. Staring at the bony monstrosities was better than staring into Halloween's eyes. The skeletons began to dance jerkily around the fire. Even the two who now only had one leg hopped about.

"Look at me," Halloween said.

I kicked at Halloween, my one damaged ankle flaring in pain. Halloween shook me hard to stop my struggling. The pain of being yanked about by my neck shot a tingle down my spine. I thought, *It'll break my neck first and then I won't feel a thing.*

"Look at me, Barry."

I did as it said. The flashing within its chest became a constant glow, illuminating its blackened heart. Halloween's eyes changed from glossy white marbles to glowing embers I couldn't look away from. Something unseen pried at the edges of my eyes and began to slip under my eyelids. It was thin and flat and cold as it worked its way under my eyelids and snaked over my eyeballs and I wasn't sure where it was going to stop but I was certain I knew how it would end . . . with my death. The tips of the snaking sensation began to probe at something further. I knew I was screaming but I couldn't hear myself and the only thing I could see was Halloween's glowing eyes and their residual glow, as if I'd been staring at the sun. I dug the tips of my fingers deep into the unnatural skin of its wrists.

Out of nowhere the cold probes retraced like an unrestrained tape measure and the light in its eyes was still fading as it dropped me on the ground. When I hit the floor so did all of Halloween's skeletal creations.

The creature turned to the tunnel leading out of the cave and snarled. Out of the darkness of the passage the sheriff appeared with Santa Claus directly behind him. The unexpected sight of Santa was thrown into an even more surreal sight by the dancing light from the fire and Halloween's illuminated chest cavity. The sheriff held his shaky hands up as if he were the one being arrested. An elf wielding a giant candy cane with a yard stake on the end to keep the cheap thing in place on a frozen yard during the holiday season appeared behind the duo and, a beat later, someone with deer antlers and a blinking red nose followed.

It took me a few seconds to realize, behind the Santa beard, it was Addisyn, wearing the moth eaten costume from our attic. Rhonda's red hair was a stark contrast to the equally as worn green elf costume. The antlers and nose Henry wore weren't as elaborate as the other two's but it was the thought that counted.

"Hey, asshole!" Addisyn shouted at Halloween.

The sheriff started and raised his hands even higher. If I weren't on the verge of death I would've reveled in his discomfort and at the dark stain on the crotch of his pants where he'd pissed himself.

"You can go now, Sheriff," Henry said. "We thank you for volunteerin' to be our guide." Henry held a butcher's knife and the knuckles of his knife-wielding hand turned white as he strengthened his grip on the weapon and stared at Halloween.

Grayson didn't need to be told twice. "I hope y'all rot in hell after yer dead," Grayson said before he disappeared back down the tunnel.

With the sheriff retreating, he exposed the pistol Addisyn had held against his back, which looked an awful like the one the sheriff carried. The same one that came in contact with my head. She refocused the aim of the weapon on Halloween.

"Come on!" Rhonda shouted at the thing. "Why don't you take one of us? Huh?"

"Even better," Henry said. "Why don't you jus' die?"

Halloween took two large strides toward the group before Addisyn began to rapidly unload the gun's contents into the creature. The thing jerked slightly with each round but bullets didn't seem to faze it. I couldn't be sure if the gun made any injuries to the thing since it's back was now to me. Halloween laughed as it continued toward the group.

Henry ran at it with his knife held high. Rhonda let loose a battle call and charged at the thing, using her candy cane like some misshaped spear. Henry reached it first but Halloween's reach was long and it backhanded Henry, knocking him off his feet. Henry lost his hold on the knife and it flew from his hand and hit the wall, ten feet from him. He lay on the ground gasping for air since the blow and subsequent fall appeared to have knocked the air out of him.

Rhonda was luckier. She'd managed to jab the pointed end of the lawn ornament upward into its stomach. Halloween hissed and grabbed at the hard, plastic candy cane but Rhonda began to jump, trying to drive it up deeper into its stomach. She was much too short to thrust it much more.

The lightning within it.

The energy to live another year.

Even if we couldn't kill it, maybe we could keep it from getting the energy it needed for another year of terror. We had to stay alive. I ripped the disgusting rabbit fur off my head and got to my feet. All my joints were overstretched and loose. My knees wobbled like a newborn fawn with each step and my ankle shot pain all the way up my leg. I noticed Henry had regained himself and was getting to his feet. Addisyn was looking around the cave in a panic, possibly for a weapon, since the gun was now empty.

Halloween let loose the most horrendous scream and knocked Rhonda to the ground. I yanked a femur bone from one of the skeletons that was barely attached by a piece of yarn. Halloween turned and grabbed at the candy cane again.

"Oh, naw you don't," Addisyn said. She leapt over Rhonda and grabbed the candy cane and jumped.

The creature squealed as the ornament went farther up into its chest. The sound of its scream was high pitched and intense and hurt my ears. I bit back the pain in my ankle and ran at Halloween. As I ran at the thing I could see the shadow of the pointed end of the candy cane silhouetted within the orange flashing chest. It was inches from the beast's blackened heart.

"The heart!" I screamed as I bashed the femur into the back of Halloween's knee.

The thing began to kneel as its knee gave out, which brought its towering form down far enough for Addisyn to give the candy cane one final thrust upward.

The cave went eerily silent except for the few shuffled steps the thing took back away from Addisyn and the crackle and pop of the echoing fire. Halloween dropped its grip from the death instrument, as did Addisyn as it stepped away from her. It went down on its knees heavily. The light within Halloween's chest flickered and stuttered a few times and began to dim.

Rhonda and Henry were now on their feet and we all watched Halloween, dumbfounded and uncertain. The creature gripped the candy cane and slid it free. Orange glowing goo dripped from the hole but quickly turned black and created a puddle.

Something in my chest fluttered like a hummingbird.

The creature turned to me and said, "I knew you'd be the one . . ." it wheezed and panted before it continued. "Are you sure you are prepared? Tonight is not for the easily scared. Creatures from hell roam on this night, for tonight is the Night of Fright." The light within it flashed bright one final time. "Trick or treat," it managed to say before collapsing to the ground and its light was forever darkened.

And everything within me finally became still.

TWENTY

IT TOOK UNTIL THE SUN came up for Henry and I to cut Halloween into pieces and burn the parts in the fire. It seemed an elaborate task with my injured ankle but I knew the people of Strang wouldn't feel completely safe until every last part of Halloween was in ashes. The thing didn't take a lot of time to burn. It was as if it were made of wood and not organic material. The flames grew taller with each part we added.

The head was last. Henry and I were covered in the black blood of Halloween by then and exhausted. A butcher's knife wasn't ideal for the job but we made it work. I lifted Halloween's heavy head and looked at it. The creature's eyes were matte and the skin was rubbery and cold. It looked no more real than a movie prop.

The girls sat on the floor near the tunnel. Rhonda's head lolled as she tried to stay awake. Addisyn had pulled the Santa beard down around her neck and was smoking a cigarette. Henry wiped his sweaty and blackened brow with his shirtsleeve.

While holding the head I told the group, "Why don't you guys get some fresh air. I'll be out in a bit."

None of them questioned me or protested. They all were eager to be done with this place and who could blame them. Once they'd retreated into the tunnel for a few seconds I tossed the head on the fire. The flames shot so high they licked the top of the cave. The head turned to ash in an instant before the ground gave way under the fire and the center collapsed and sunk like the sand of an hourglass, plummeting the cave into complete darkness.

I spotted the pinprick of light from the outside at the end of the tunnel and limped my way toward it. Once I emerged I found myself in the middle of a harvested cornfield. The other three were lying on the grass hill covering the disguised tunnel's entrance. Grayson was nowhere to be seen.

"How'd Grayson know where this was?" I said.

Rhonda sat up and gave me a worn and sly smile. "Guess it's his job to be nosey."

Henry and Addisyn stood and began to make their way down the grassy strip separating two cornfields. The path led to a beat-up car I recognized as Rhonda's. Rhonda and I walked side by side behind the other two, she kept pace with my slow progress.

Rhonda said, "I ran straight to your house to get the other two. Couldn't imagine what I was thinkin' when I saw them dressin' up." She giggled.

I ignored her. There were more pressing things on my mind.

Henry said, "Guess it wasn't afraid of Christmas."

"Guess not," Addisyn said. She finally pulled the Santa hat from her head and stripped off the beard.

Rhonda looked at me expectantly and shyly. "That's it then, huh?"

Before, I would've been too embarrassed to talk to her. But all of that was trivial now. I knew what she wanted from me and it was a little too late. I said, "Until next Halloween."

"Next Halloween?" She looked at me confused.

"There ain't gonna be another festival," Addisyn said before lighting a cigarette. "I quit."

"Me too," Henry said.

No one said anything else. The only sound accompanying our trek to the car was our footfalls through the overgrown and dewy dried autumn grass. There would be a next year with or without them. Because I could feel my still heart growing cold and black.

Other Grindhouse Press Titles

Made in the USA
Las Vegas, NV
28 August 2023

76761527R00069